Frisky Business
Flight Crew Book 1
RM Bellamy

This is for all the people feeling stuck in unsupportive relationships. There's more out there. Don't be afraid to push past the discomfort and go after what you want. Sometimes turning your world upside down has to happen to set things right.

Author's Note

I don't work in an airport. I only write about them. So just live in the delusion with me.

TROPES, TAGS, and CONTENT WARNINGS

Blurb Hayes Collins has put his days of romance behind him. As a single dad with a grown daughter, he's not looking for anyone to intrude on the quiet mountain life he leads when he's not working as the head DHS agent for the Charlotte International Airport.

But when he detains the beautiful and curvaceous Millie for carrying illegal substances, his life takes a sudden turn. Even when she's found innocent, he's reluctant to let the younger beauty out of his sight. He's more interested in leading her straight to his bed.

TROPES Happily ever after, insta-lust, insta-love, airport security, age-gap romance, soulmates, one night stand turns into more.

TAGS HEA guaranteed, age-gap, airport romance, please don't take me to your cabin to kill me, this guy should definitely not be in charge, standard procedure my ass, strip search, get frisked, light breeding kink, light dom dynamics, single dad, widower, Daddy vibes, might as well be a whore, put a baby in me, ass virgin, is it too big, dog dad, cat mom, Charlotte, NC.

CONTENT WARNINGS This book is lighthearted, for the most part. However, because Hayes is a widower, there is brief mention of loss of spouse and parent on page But the death is not shown, as it happened many years prior to the start of the story. Likewise, there is a brief mention of drugs.

There are graphic scenes of sexual nature in this book. Some have called them vanilla. But I know others will still blush. Proceed at your own risk.

Playlist

Guilty Pleasure - Chappell Roan
Heartlines (MOUNT Remix) - BROODS, MOUNT
Mastermind - Taylor Swift
Invisible String - Taylor Swift
Guilty as Sin? - Taylor Swift
The Alchemy - Taylor Swift
You Are In Love - Taylor Swift
Vertigo - Griff
Easy to Love - Armin van Buuren, Matoma, Teddy Swims
Better - Billy Raffoul
Thinking 'Bout Love - Wild Rivers, Wrabel
What You're Running From - Jamie Gray
Hold Me - Teddy Swims
Feather - Sabrina Carpenter
Juno - Sabrina Carpenter
Your Bones - Chelsea Cutler

1

Hayes

It's a normal morning by my standards. Too many people. My coworkers are too chipper. I haven't had enough coffee. I'm dreading heading downstairs into the madness of Checkpoint E. Barring anyone trying to screw around today, these people will soon be out of my hair and on the way to their destinations.

But there's always one person, isn't there?

I look down into the crowd, around and over the heads of people, trying to decipher who it'll be. The guy in sweatpants holding on to a ratty gym bag? Bless the people standing next to him. As he coughs into the sleeve of his jacket, I take an automatic step back as if whatever germs he's harboring will reach me.

Or maybe the problem will be the woman six people back with the pet carrier? Who knows what's in there? Could be a cat. Or a puppy. I've seen stranger things. Last week, a kid tried to walk his bearded dragon through the scanner on a leash.

I keep looking down the line until I reach a woman and man who stand next to each other but are otherwise not interacting. The woman stands a little ahead, looking at her phone. Brunette. Shoulder-length hair down around her face. Late twenties to early thirties, maybe. Roughly five foot seven inches, if I'm right—and I'm hardly ever wrong about those things. It's hard for me not to assess people. It's what I've been trained to do—it's what I'm good at. Sometimes, though, I get stuck on a certain aspect.

Right now, I'm stuck on her overall demeanor. She's beautiful. Effortlessly so. Maybe it's the fluorescent lights playing tricks on me. Or maybe the people next to her are exceptionally unfortunate looking.

I can't look away from *her*. Her curves are contained in a pair of black leggings, a bright yellow crop top, and a gray sweatshirt wrapped around her waist. Yeah, her natural beauty is clear, but that's not what immediately draws my attention.

There's something about how she's turned away from the man right now—how her shoulders hunch over.

It's when the man beside her casually slips something into the side of her backpack and then taps her shoulder that my attention finally drifts up to her face.

She's annoyed.

She looks at him and frowns, crossing her arms over her ample chest. But then he steps in front of her and crowds her in, blocking my view of her reaction.

And suddenly I'm on edge. Call it cautious paranoia after being in this job for over two decades, or a gut feeling. Looking in the right place at the right time. Call it whatever you want.

Looks like we might have some fun today. Even if it is just rescuing a woman in distress.

People may be stupid, but the outgoing terminal of the Charlotte airport isn't usually where people try anything. People do dumb shit. Sometimes we get an idiot who tries to do something stupid in security, thinking they're above the system. Most of the time, it's not even dangerous—except when it is.

Just last week, the TSA guys had a mom try to send her kid down the belt into the scanner with her kid buckled into the car seat. When they went to flip it over, because of protocol, they realized the kid was in there. Arguing ensued, and there was a bit of a show. I haven't seen any car seats yet this morning.

My German Shepherd, Bruno, shifts beside me. We've been here an hour already. He's done his business and I've had my first cup of black coffee and finished my reports from yesterday. The only thing left to do? Go downstairs and face the crowds. From my spot overlooking the security area, I push off the banister and head for the stairs.

"Come on, buddy. Let's get to work."

2

Millie

Travel days suck. Whoever thought it would be a good idea to schedule a flight at 6:30 in the morning should be punched in the face. You have to be at the airport at least two hours early.

Forget checking bags. Better make it three hours. And if you live more than half an hour away from this side of town, you have to plan for travel time. You want to make sure you give yourself plenty of time to get through security, too. Which is where I'm at currently.

Standing behind at least two hundred people, queued up, waiting for our turn to half undress ourselves and walk under the giant body scanners.

Thankfully, I wore socks and slip-on shoes today. I've made the mistake of going without socks once or twice and could only think about the germs on my body for the rest of the day. I look around me at everyone in sandals and flip-flops, their bare toes about to touch the nasty airport linoleum floor.

I'm already sweating, trying my best to hide the fact from the dozens of people standing in my vicinity. I don't want to be *that* person in line. The one you can smell by just looking at them. Then again, I think that job's been taken by the guy with the gym bag, three people behind me.

I'm killing time on my phone, watching the line movement carefully, so I'm not the one responsible for holding it up. It's moving faster than usual today. The customer service agent at baggage drop told us it might. *The dogs are out*, they said. And they weren't lying. A few different breeds and their handlers walk the perimeter of the lines. The dogs are sniffing while the agents stroll with their eyes on us all. Another agent and his dog stand near the TSA booths, allowing two people at a time to cross over into the security area. At this rate, it'll be our turn soon.

But Jon isn't a patient person. While I have patience in droves—being a second-grade teacher—I have no tolerance for his special brand of asshole this morning. Hell, I don't even know why I'm on this trip to his hometown in Texas in the first place. I had to take a week off from both my jobs to do this, and be at the airport super early because the first flight was the only time of day his mom could pick us up at the other end.

A tap on my shoulder stirs me from my thoughts, and I turn my attention to the man in question. Rather, the thorn in my side. "Yeah?"

I pocket my phone as he crowds me into the ropes behind me.

"When we get to Dallas, Todd is picking me up, and we're going over to the gym. You're going to have to sit at my mom's and help her." He types on his phone, not bothering to look at me as he talks. Even if he did, he wouldn't truly *see* me. I'm not sure he ever has.

I groan internally. I knew this was going to happen. It happens every time. And every time I try to get out of it, he comes up with an excuse, and I cave. I have half a mind to leave this line, grab a taxi back to the apartment, and just enjoy the time off by myself. His mom and I don't get along. We never have. Never will. I don't get along with his friends either.

I'm not even sure why we're still together. It's purely out of comfort at this point. And not even the good kind. It's like the kind that you keep around because the unknown is worse. At least the monster I know is predictable. The crumbs I've come to expect are better than none.

Rubbing at my forehead, I go to take a step back. But where there was a rope before, now there's a wall. A warm, sturdy, muscular wall that smells just slightly of pine.

"Excuse me. Is there a problem?" the wall asks in a gruff voice, placing a hand on my lower back to stop me from falling on my ass.

"No. Just telling my girlfriend our plans for the day once we land," Jon says. I turn to speak but falter when I have to look up to meet the kind yet intense dark blue eyes of a DHS agent. Not TSA, I note, taking in the large letters on his vest, and his dog, a German Shepherd with the most beautiful sable coat. But why have they singled us out?

Mr. Tall, Blue-eyed, and Buff doesn't move. The dog starts pulling on the leash, his nose in the air, aimed in my direction. I quickly shake my head as Jon says "no."

"If there's no problem, you both won't mind stepping out of line and allowing my dog to search you both real quick," he states, his words clear and void of confusion. While he's not asking us, there's a hint of kindness behind the deep timbre of his voice.

It's *manly* and sends a shiver from the nape of my neck down my back, an unfamiliar warmth flooding my senses. I'm ready to duck under the rope and do as he says. Besides the tone in his voice that demands my compliance, you never argue with security. Or anyone who works for or at the airport. Hell, I just want to ask him if I can go home. This is ridiculous.

As I grab the handle of my carry-on, Jon stops me with a hand on my wrist. "We're about to go through the scanners. They'll search us then if there's an issue."

"Son, that wasn't a question."

Son. I take a deep breath at the use of the word. Jon doesn't have a great relationship with his dad. Not that this man knows that. He's clearly older. How much older, I'm not sure. From the gray hair at his temples and sprinkled throughout his clipped beard to the slight wrinkles surrounding his eyes, it's hard to tell. And why am I focused on it? The man's only trying to do his job.

"Grab your things and step over here to the side." He unlatches the rope and gestures for us to move.

I've never moved quicker in my life. I have nothing to hide. Let the dog sniff. The only thing they'll come up with is the smell of my two cats, Latte and Orca. Just thinking of the two stinkers has me wanting to snuggle up with them. My sister has them for the week, and I know they're in good hands.

"Collins to the operator. I need a female agent at Checkpoint E, ASAP. I repeat. Female agent to Checkpoint E. Over." He speaks into the radio attached to his shoulder and it's then I notice the name tag velcroed to his vest. *H. Collins*.

What does the "H" stand for? *Handsome? Hot? Handsy?* Or maybe his parents gave him a more traditional name like Hunter or Harrison.

A minute later, a shorter female agent, dressed similarly to Collins but without a dog, ambles up to us and smirks. "Are we taking this upstairs?"

"Not yet, Smitty. Haven't even let Bruno here at 'em." On that note, he loosens his hold on the dog's leash, and they step closer to us. Bruno sniffs at the ground, making his way to our feet, and then to our bags. When he lingers a little longer near me, sniffing once, then twice at my backpack, I nervously chuckle and take it off, gently placing it at my feet.

"I have two cats... he probably smells those."

"Oh, sweetie. They don't alert us to other animals." *Smitty* kneels to the ground and gestures to the backpack before pulling a pair of blue latex gloves out of her front pants pocket. "I'm going to need to look in here."

I get a quick look at her name tag.

J. Smith.

I shrug my shoulders at her statement, not sure what I'm supposed to do. Say "go for it"? "No, please don't!"? Agent Collins crosses his arms and stands back.

What the hell is happening? Do these dogs sniff out birth control pills and Prozac? That's all that's in there.

Except, when she pulls out a small, unfamiliar bag and holds it in the air, I know it's time to panic. Because that's not mine. But I know what it is, who it belongs to, and I know who put it there.

3

Hayes

Well, it looks like my skills aren't waning. *Cats, my ass.* It's always the innocent-looking ones, isn't it?

Bruno keeps sniffing around, but when he doesn't alert me to anything else, I pull him back to sit in an alert position at my feet, taking a treat out of my pocket and feeding it to him discreetly.

"Are you two traveling together?" I ask, already knowing the answer.

"Yes!" the woman shouts just as the man takes a step back and says "no."

"Let me see your tickets and IDs." I hold out my hand. Again, it's not a question. She hands me hers quickly while he fumbles through his pocket for his. I may have seen him put something in her bag, but I still have to play this out until we get actual answers.

"Millicent-Rose Anderson and Jon Hildegard? For two people not traveling together, wanna tell me why you live at the same address? Or why two seconds ago she was your girlfriend and now you don't know her?" I pocket both the tickets and IDs and gesture for one of my agents to hurry over.

"Take these to my office, please." The younger man nods his head and starts collecting their bags.

"Wait!" Jon shouts. "We have a flight to catch. That wasn't in my bag. I've done nothing wrong. I'm just trying to fly home to visit family. Can't I just... go? It's not like it's a bomb! Which, by the way, isn't that all they're supposed to sniff out?" he pleads. But I shake my head as Millicent punches his arm.

Things are rarely as cut and dry as they seem, and I'm willing to bet that Little Miss Innocent Millicent Rose isn't exactly as innocent as she'd like me to believe. This guy is just the tip of the iceberg of what there is to know about her.

"Sounds like someone did their research," my agent, Jenna Smith, remarks, turning her back to the couple.

"We're going upstairs. You can go quietly, or we can handcuff you and force you up there." I pat the handcuffs that sit in a holster around my waist.

"The sooner we get this handled, the sooner you'll be on your way. But I hate to say, you should probably make some calls. Because marijuana isn't allowed in airports and especially not on planes—not in North Carolina, at least—and I have questions for you both."

Millicent nods her head and raises her hands. "Just take me where you want me to go."

And gods above, why am I immediately plagued with the image of her in my handcuffs, bent over my bed? That's what my dick wants. Her compliance does something to me. I want to smile, sit down, pull her down in my lap, and teach her a lesson. Regardless of where my thoughts are straying, I'm going to punch this idiot boyfriend of hers and then spank her.

Because how can she date him? And why, for the love of god, am I having these thoughts?

I run my free hand over my face, hiding a grunt.

"Please. I'll do whatever it is you want. But I haven't done anything wrong. I don't know how that got there." She bites at her bottom lip and tears well in her green eyes. She's tired. And to have this be the first thing to deal with in the morning? I feel for her. I do. She's scared. Her so-called "boyfriend," though? He's acting as if this is a nuisance.

"Let's get you both upstairs and away from prying eyes." It's not the guy I'm worried about. I don't want people looking at her or thinking she did something wrong. Knowing that we still have to go through with the standard protocol, I want her in a private space. We gather up the rest of their things, each take hold of an arm, and direct them to the set of stairs. I've got a hold of Jon, but take a look over my shoulder to watch Jenna and Millicent carefully.

If I'm not careful, I'll give away the fact I'm playing favorites. But honestly, let the asshole find out I'm being nicer to his girl. She shouldn't be his girl anyway.

Getting upstairs, I shove Jon in the first interrogation room. "Wait here." I beep him in, then make sure the door is locked again after it latches. I can feel Jenna's eyes on my back as I proceed to the next empty room, raise my badge to the scanner, and beep the three of us in.

"This is standard procedure, Millicent. We need to pat you down, and then I'll leave you with Agent Smith to answer some questions." Pointing to the metal table in the middle of the room, I gesture for her to stay standing. "This will only take a second."

Wrapped up in knowing my hand is millimeters from her body, I don't even stop to issue her a warning or to ask if there's anything sharp on her person. And yet, while I know what I'm doing is stupid, I proceed with little to no caution for my own well-being, as if the thought of not getting my hands on her immediately is the biggest safety concern of them all.

Millicent's arms are folded in on herself, hugging her stomach, shoulders hunched over. I hate this—I do—but it has to be done. My hand slowly snakes out and guides her into place. "Hands on the table, feet shoulder-width apart." I have to run my hand down the expanse of her back and over her hips to situate her.

"Hayes, what do you think you're doing?" Jenna yanks on my arm, pulling me out of the way so she can get in between me and Millicent.

I have no idea what I'm doing.

I let the smaller woman push me as if I weigh nothing and back up against the wall, hands up in defense. Millicent stands still with her hands on the table, fingers pulled under her palms, tense. Her legs are spread apart and she's got her head tilted down. Despite the commotion, she's frozen.

And I had a part in that.

Shit.

"Get out of here and go to your office or something. You crossed the line. If I'd have known you were going to actually start patting her down..." Jenna shakes her head at me as she points to the door. "I'm glad I was here."

"I didn't..." I lower my voice, running a hand over the back of my head. "Millicent, I'm so sorry..."

"Oh, get frisked," The power of Millicent's biting voice from over her shoulder sends a chill down my spine and straight to my dick.

She heard the conversation between me and Jenna. Of course she did. We're standing in a room the size of a sardine can.

As to what Jenna said? I'll leave the room. But I'm not going to my office.

4

Millie

Whatever the hell that was, I'm glad it's over. Except—I inhale deeply, steadying myself.

Shit. Motherfucking shit, dirtbag, asshole. I'm not sure what to do about how my mind and body are reeling from the aftereffects of his touch.

"I'm sorry about that, Ms. Anderson. What he should have said is that we have to do a quick pat down before we start. And that I'll be handling it. Do you have anything sharp on your body?"

I close my eyes and shake my head, unable to give her a verbal answer. And when her gloved hands start their ascent up my legs, over my arms, and around my front, I tense, expecting it to feel similar if not the same to Hayes's touch. I'm not sure if there are enough deep breaths that will calm me, but thankfully, the movement of her hands is soon done. Despite her quick job, my hands uncurl from their fists and slip against the tabletop.

"Take a seat over there. Do you need any water?" she asks, pulling off her gloves and tossing them into the trashcan by the door. Even though I have cottonmouth and could take down a gallon of water right about now, I decline it with a shake of my head. I'm on the verge of tears, but I won't cry. Not with her in the room.

Sitting down, I crane my neck to the far upper corners and spy two cameras. One is trained on me, behind her, and one is on her, from behind me. A mirror, one-way if I'm guessing, is embedded in the wall to my left. This is my first time in an interrogation room. But I've watched enough TV to know they didn't put this in here so I could use it to apply my lip gloss.

"Well, then. Let's get started. It's actually standard procedure for me to do a strip search." She pulls out the chair opposite me and slides into it gracefully.

"A—I'm sorry... a—" Okay. Well, I didn't plan on crying. But now? I know what that means. And I'm not okay with that. "Agent... Smith... I..."

"Ms. Anderson." One corner of her lips ticks upward. "I'm joking. Listen..." She leans forward on the table, folding her hands into one another just in front of herself.

"What?" She's *joking?* "Agent Smith. That's a terrible joke." I lay my head down on the table and laugh out a sigh of relief, but it's immediately followed by anger. "He—"

Hayes. "He knew the whole time?"

"Believe me when I say that this is nothing in comparison to how your boyfriend is being treated in the next room. Are you sure you don't need anything?"

"My backpack?" I ask, hopeful. My phone is in there.

"Unfortunately, no." That's the only answer I get. "I'm going to check on things and then will bring you back a coffee and water." She gets up and leaves the small room.

I'm left to stand and make my way over to the mirror. If I'm going to be left alone, I might as well fix my hair. I can't help but feel like I'm being watched by more than just the cameras, though.

5

Hayes

"Why'd you have to start her off like that, Jenna?" My co-worker slips into the room quietly, and I turn to see her smirking. That damn smirk. I just want to wipe it clear off her face most of the time. She's great at her job. Hardly gives me any trouble. But she toes the line of testing me, for sure.

Like now.

She disappeared, leaving Millicent in the room by herself. And the girl looked at herself in the one-way mirror, not realizing I looked right back. Unashamedly. With abandon.

For the first time since pulling her and her boyfriend upstairs, I let my eyes linger over her curves from close up. The same curves Jenna just frisked. While I wish it had been me doing the frisking, we have protocols in place for a reason at work. But now I'm fantasizing about every inch of her that my friend touched. How, when Millicent used her hair tie to pull her hair up, it immediately drew more attention to her lips somehow. She pursed them together in concentration as she worked her hair up in its messy knot.

Right now, she's leaning back in her chair, arched against the backrest. More than an inch of her stomach peeks out from her cropped shirt, giving me just the smallest peek of a simple black sports bra. It's enough to send my pulse racing.

"Because sometimes it's fun to watch the innocent ones squirm too." Jenna stands next to me at the window. "Get enough of an eyeful there, boss?"

"I..." I should correct her. But it's no use.

"It's okay, Hayes." Jenna slaps me on the back. She's about a foot and a half shorter than me. What she lacks in height, she makes up for in brute force. She's former military, and the rest of the guys know not to mess with her. Unfortunately, other guys, like Jon, don't. She looks innocent but could kill you with her pinky. She's my secret weapon in a petite, blonde package. Working with her day in and day out is nothing, I'm sure, compared to dating her or living with her. God bless her partner. Or is it partners? She hasn't updated me this month.

"It's really not okay." There's something about the woman in the room behind this one-way mirror that has me wanting to throw her over my shoulder and high-tail it out of here, drive her to my cabin, and keep her locked away from the world for the foreseeable future. Hell. I have enough PTO saved up; I could disappear for months, and no one would bat an eye. This woman looks like she needs to be ravished six ways to Sunday. I could be the man for the job. If I didn't have fucking morals and ethics.

"You've never…?" Jenna makes a crude gesture with her hands and thrusts her hips at the empty air.

"Didn't you say you were going to get water and coffee?" I side-eye her, tilting my chin down to my chest, not bothering to answer that question.

We've worked together for too long, gotten too comfortable with one another. I should have asked a rookie to come handle Millicent. One whose favorite hobby isn't reading every single one of my micro-expressions and then making fun of me for them. This is going to be a longer morning now that we have to wait for someone from the city to come and detain Jon. And I intend to make sure Millicent gets home safely. Preferably not to the same place she left this morning, even if that means I have to take her to a hotel. Jenna would kill me if she knew what I was really thinking.

6

Hayes

"Took you long enough…" Douche-canoe mutters as I close the door to the interrogation room. He's reclined in his seat, too comfortable for the situation. Either he thinks he's off the hook, or he doesn't care. From his apathetic behavior downstairs, I'm going to assume somewhere between the two.

"I'm sorry?" I turn to him, not trying to hide the amusement in my voice, and raise a brow. "Did we leave you waiting too long? Did we interrupt your morning? Unless I'm mistaken," I start and make my way over to the table. I flip the chair around and straddle it, sitting in it backward. "You are the one I saw sneak this little guy into your girlfriend's backpack this morning."

I've already pulled the evidence bag from my outer vest pocket and now wave it in his face. I don't need him to admit the truth. That's for the cops to handle. I saw him with my own eyes. Besides, his fingerprints will be on the bag.

"I don't know what you think you saw from up there on your golden platform, looking down..."

"What I saw"—I lean forward, keeping hold of the bag—"was you, taking *this* and sliding it ever so gently into the front pocket of Millicent's backpack." The closer I lean, the more he backs up, leaning back in his chair. "Then you tapped her on her shoulder to get her attention. She didn't like that very much."

My chest tightens under my vest and I do my best in the moment to cool my facial expression and not furl my fists on top of the table. "Now, I'm sure I know why you slipped it in there. You saw the dogs. You panicked. Thought, 'Hey, I'm about to go on vacation. I accidentally left this in my bag. There's no trash can around... Damn it... Oh, wait... my girlfriend's backpack will do.' I'll give you a solid C+ for effort, James. Really."

"You're an asshole," he scoffs, turning to look at the door.

"No one's coming to save you. In fact, the next people through that door are gonna be a couple officers who will take you down to the city station and handle it from there." Jon shakes his head. "And as for what the dogs sniff for…" I recall his earlier statement and take a second to scratch at my beard. "That's none of your business."

"It is my business, though. You searched my shit, and now you're holding me here illegally."

"I would never." And that's mostly the truth. I'm pretty damn captivated by a woman after hardly a conversation that I'm willing to bet I'd hold him here for over the limit if she batted her eyelashes at me the right way. And that's dangerous. No woman has had me like this. Not even the women I've had the occasional hookups with over the years since my kid moved out. Or the years following my wife's passing. But this incident has me rethinking my whole life. I'm instantly on guard for a woman I don't know.

What is this shit?

A knock at the door startles me, and Jenna walks in. "Hey, Collins. The other one is asking for you." She gestures with her head to the interrogation room next to this one, where Millicent sits.

She's asking for *me*? Whether or not this is a good or bad thing, it doesn't matter. I'm already on my feet and to the door.

"You don't have to stay here with him." I nod to Jon. "The cops will be here in a few minutes."

Jenna follows me, shuts the door behind us, and walks the few steps over to the other room with me, leaning in to whisper. "She's pissed that you called them both out like that when you *knew* she didn't do anything wrong."

We're standing toe to toe, my hand now on the doorknob as Jenna lifts her badge to the scanner and beeps me in.

"Yeah. I know," I mutter as I walk in, not remotely ready to face the music.

7
Millie

gent Hayes Collins. In the flesh. Standing at the door. Is he waiting for me to say something?

"Jenna got you coffee and water. Good." He casually walks over to the table and joins me, sitting down, placing his hands palms down on the table in front of him.

"Yeah." Small talk. Cool. "I'm—"

"Millicent, I'm sorry…" We both speak at the same time.

"About what?" I ask. "About *arresting* me after knowing I didn't do anything wrong? Or *keeping* me here after knowing I didn't do anything wrong? Which part?"

"You haven't been arrested." He chuckles dryly and wipes at his mouth. "I did have to detain you though. You understand that, right? We found drugs on your person. Even if he put them there."

"That didn't save me from the embarrassment, Hay—I mean, Agent Collins..." I can't believe I just almost first-named a federal agent. And by the way he's looking at me, he can't believe it either. He stares at me blankly, blue eyes wide, hands splayed on the table. He blinks once, then twice before standing up straight to his full height.

"Millicent..."

"That was an accident. I'm sorry." I apologize. "Please don't..."

"Please don't what?" I'm not expecting him to walk to my side of the table, kneel down, and meet me at eye level. "I'm not mad, Millicent." One hand lands on the back of the chair, and the other crowds mine on the table. He doesn't touch me, despite the lack of distance between my pinky and his index finger.

"I'm mad. Even if you aren't. Who is in charge here? How is it that you can just pull people out of security when you *know* they didn't do anything wrong?" I wait to see if he answers for himself. When it looks as if he isn't going to, I continue to the reason why I'm livid. "If my work finds out what happened here today... I could—I could lose my job and... I can't..."

I'm too close to a panic attack in this small, musty room with this handsome stranger. I use my feet on the ground to back away from the table with force.

"Whoa, Millie." The way he shortens my name, it sounds like he's calming a horse. "Like I said, you're not under arrest." I flinch as his hand lands on my shoulder.

Gentle. Warm. Just enough weight to keep me grounded. Because I'm still two-point-five seconds from flying off the handle. He picks up my water bottle on the table, and hands it to me with his free hand. "Drink this, and then we'll talk about when you can leave." I do as he says. "Is there someone we can call for you?" He hasn't moved his hand. It still rests on my shoulder. "Your parents? A friend?"

My parents? For god's sake. "I'm an adult, Agent Collins." I roll my eyes.

"I'm sorry, Millicent-Rose Anderson. Did you just roll your eyes at me?" He inches slightly closer to me and lowers his voice. "I merely asked you if we could call someone. It's a yes or a no answer. Followed up by a series of numbers and a name. I'm trying to help you."

"Are you this frisky with all of your prisoners?"

"I swear..." The man literally growls, stands up, and leaves the room.

8

Hayes

I replay the end of that conversation in my head. I had to get out of there. She was testing me with the eye roll and the brattiness. The answer was no. Of course, I'm not *this frisky* with all of my *detainees*. But hell if I don't want to get frisky with her. And, if I didn't know any better, I'd say she knows what she's doing. But she's simply out of sorts. *Right?*

I walk to my office, where Bruno is lying on the futon against the wall. His ears perk up at hearing me but he quickly settles when I wave my hand in a downward motion. I spy her backpack beside my desk, reach for it, and carry it with me back to the interrogation room. My guys should have already searched the bags. There's a report on my desk. I'll look at it later. Right now, I need to be honest with the pissed-off woman who I left sitting by herself and see if we can work on getting her home and maybe opening up to me while she's still here.

When I walk in with her bag, she's staring at the table. She doesn't look up. And I'm not surprised. I know what we did was wrong. But the part of me that needs, that wants, to take care of her? He doesn't care. I throw the bag on the table. Some of the contents rattle.

It's then she looks up and gasps. "Agent Smith said I couldn't have my bag." Without waiting for my permission, she reaches for it, snatching it into her arms. In the front pocket, she finds her cell phone.

"Agent Smith isn't the boss. I am."

"You're shitting me." She's not letting this go. Looking up to meet my gaze, she stares at me with hardened eyes. Earlier, she was scared. Her lips trembled as we stood outside of security, and she told us to take her away. Now? She's mad and has gained back her resolve. I like the gumption. "And this is the kind of operation you're running around here?"

"I don't expect you to understand how this normally works, Millicent."

"Quit first-naming me like we're friends, Hayes!" she shouts right back at me, almost leaping from the chair.

"What in the hell, woman? Who pissed in your corn-flakes this morning?" I take hold of her arms and hold her in her seat. Gumption or not, things have gotten out of control if she thinks she can talk to me like this. She's seconds away from spitting in my face or slapping me. And at this point? I'm not sure either wouldn't turn me on further.

Her heavy breathing draws me in, and I'm inches from doing something really stupid. The warm puffs fanning me have me swaying on my feet. But my grip on her arms only tightens. She's grounding me as much as I'm attempting to ground her.

"Hayes..." My name leaves her lips in a whisper. I slowly release my hands, each finger unfurling intentionally.

"I thought you were going to run away. I'm sorry I grabbed a hold of you." I walk over to the second chair, putting some much-needed distance between us.

If Jenna watches the video later, she's going to laugh at this whole interaction. The back and forth, me grabbing our detainee. And I probably shouldn't tell the brunette beauty in front of me this. Yet I do, pointing to the two cameras, one with each index finger. "I'm going to get hell for that later, anyway. Jenna, I mean Agent Smith, watches the feed on her lunch breaks. So I'll stay over here if you can promise me not to try and escape."

I stare at her, watching to see what her next move will be.

She moves to lean forward on the table, resting her chin on top of folded fingers. "I'm pretty sure that door is locked. Just like I'm sure that mirror is actually a window."

"Not wrong," I mutter. "Any other observations? What's your day job? You wanna come work for me?" It's a joke, one she picks up on.

"I teach second grade in Huntersville. And on the weekends, I work at a coffee shop. Unfortunately, I don't have time for a third job, so I'll have to decline that invitation. As enticing as it may be." Her eyes dip down for a moment. Am I delusional, or did she just give me a once-over?

I didn't miss the part where she mentioned *two jobs*.

I'm impressed and upset.

It appears she's overworking herself. If she's working multiple jobs and her boyfriend sits at home on his ass, I won't be able to keep my mouth shut.

I'm not one of those guys who wants his woman at home: cooking, cleaning, barefoot and pregnant. Though, the thought of that is more than nice.

I'm immediately overtaken by the image of her standing on the porch of my cabin in a white sundress, waiting for me as I turn down the gravel drive, toddler on her hip and her belly swollen with another one of our babies.

But, *hell*. What am I thinking? I'm an old man. She has so much life left to live. I'm already a father to one adult kid. What will my daughter say if I bring Millie home and make this vision come true?

I'm fucked. I'm having thoughts that I need to shut down before I carry her out of here and to my office, lock us in there, and make her mine, putting my handcuffs to use from my earlier vision.

"You're being awfully quiet now. Didn't mean to offend you by declining that job offer." She smirks. "Are you that hard up for untrained, unfiltered, thirty-one-year-old women in the DHS?"

"Honey, that's not why I'm silent over here." I wipe my hand over my clipped beard, down my neck, running it back around to rest on my nape. There really is no reason for me to keep her here any longer, is there? "You're free to go."

"That's it?"

I stand up and help her gather her things. To hell with protocol. If I don't get her out of here now, I'm going to break.

"I'll show you back downstairs. I can't guarantee you they got your bags before they made it to the plane. But we can check with the desk agents downstairs." I've got her backpack slung over my shoulder, my hand already twisting the doorknob as I scan my ID to exit.

Then she's behind me and pushing the door shut. "What just happened? You were ready to keep me here 'til the sun set, and then..."

"Do you want to leave or not?" I ask in a curt tone, my breath barely controlled. "The amount of marijuana we found on you was barely enough to warrant arresting him.

And I saw with my own eyes as he put it in your bag," I admit.

She's standing at my shoulder, and from where I'm looking down, my gaze hits the top of her head. She looks up through her thick lashes in confusion. That's the only word to call it. *Well*, both of us are confused.

"Nothing happened, Millicent. Let go of the door." I use my authoritative tone and watch as she slowly lowers her arm. "Just follow me and don't talk to anyone. Okay? Can you listen and do that?" I'm not even a few hours into my workday, and I'm already about to call it quits.

We enter the hall, and I take a look around before ushering her out in front of me.

As soon as she steps across the threshold, the door to the other room opens, and Jon is pushed out by Jenna and two uniformed officers. The scumbag looks up and stops in his tracks.

"Keep moving," Jenna urges him with a hand on his shoulder, his arms handcuffed behind his back.

"Why aren't you taking her downtown?" he shouts over his other shoulder, fighting the cops and Jenna as they continue dragging him down the hall.

Before I can stop her, she marches up to him. The cops stop, and Jenna takes a step back. I can't see the look on Millicent's face. But from behind, her walk screams determination, with her fists furled at her side and her feet stomping on the ground.

When she rears back her hand and slaps him across the face, I hold back a laugh. Jenna barks out a laugh but immediately draws her fist to her lips to cover her mistake. I cross my arms and watch this unfold. Millie needs to get this out of her system.

"We're done." She turns on her heels and marches back over to me.

"No one is gonna say or do anything? You're gonna let that bitch assault me?" Jon cries.

With Jenna still controlling her laughter, one of the officers speaks up.

"Let's go." He grabs hold of Jon and continues down the hall.

"This way, Millie." I'm a little more than bothered by her display of dominance just now. And not in a bad way. In dragging her down the hall, we end up in my office, which is the one place I shouldn't have brought her. When the door shuts, and we're standing alone—Bruno snoring on the couch—I back up against the door.

"Well, that just happened."

"Ugh. He's—I should have done that so long ago. But I couldn't. We've..." She spins around and throws herself on the couch next to my dog. He stirs but otherwise ignores her. "Why am I telling you any of this? You're not my friend. You're not my therapist."

"You're right. But I'm here and willing to listen. We can wait for them to leave, and then I'll get you out of here." I cross the floor and take a seat behind my desk, throwing one leg over the other as I watch her carefully. She's fidgeting with the hem of her cropped shirt again and looking at Bruno.

"You can pet him. He won't bite you. He's off duty for the moment."

"So if he were on duty, he'd bite me?" She looks between me and my dog with a raised brow. But it doesn't take long before she snakes a hand through his fur and up to his head, where she scratches behind his ears. In a matter of seconds, he's moved his head to her lap, and she's relaxed a bit more.

"Do we need to order you a car? Or can a family member pick you up?" The longer we wait, the longer I'll sit with these feelings. And I don't need my dog getting too comfortable with her, either.

"I don't—" she starts. "We brought Jon's truck. I don't have the keys. And honestly..."

"I can't give you the keys." I look at Jon's things next to my desk and shake my head. "So, family or car service?"

9

Millie

"*So, family or car service?*"

Neither of those options works for me. Yes, if I call my sister, she'll come get me. That is, after she complains for half an hour how this is a major inconvenience. Then I'll have to pay for her gas. And a car service? That's way more expensive. Where would they take me? I'm sure as hell not going to the apartment.

"I can practically see the wheels turning in your head." Hayes leans forward on his elbows, eyeing me. I feel trapped under his stare, in his office, surrounded by his things. His scent? It's homey. Almost *too* homey. I'd have no problem curling up with a blanket and falling asleep in here, knowing I'm safe and sound. Hell. I think if he was with me anywhere, I could doze off. Hayes and Bruno, looking out for me. "Lay it out for me."

"If I call my sister, she'll just be mad at me. And it will be a whole thing. Plus, she was looking forward to a whole week with my cats. And... I can't take that away from her." I can't give her nieces or nephews any time soon. Cats are the only substitute. He only nods his head.

"Okay. What about your parents?"

"They live too far away," I respond, not giving him any specifics.

"Okay. Well, we need to get you home. So I'll schedule a car for you. We can use my airport discount if money's an issue." He goes to pull his desk phone towards him, but I shake my head.

"I can't go back to that apartment. I mean... I could. I have a key. But I'm not ready." I scrunch up my face, twisting my lips in disgust. I could go, pack a bag, and head to my sister's house before Jon ever gets home.

"Millie." I'm not expecting the emotions that stir in me when he shortens my name—a blend of tenderness mixed with trepidation, leaving me somehow feeling secure. I sit up straighter on the couch. "You have to give me something to work with here. You can't sit at the airport all day. And unfortunately, I can't just let you on another flight: standard procedure." There's an exasperation to his tone.

"Standard procedure, my ass," I huff, removing my hand from Bruno's back. The dog whines briefly at the loss of contact but quickly replaces his head in my lap. "Tom

Hanks lived in that airport for... what? Months, right? I can stay here for a week." Agent *Standard Procedure* has the nerve to laugh.

"Well, now that I know your plan, I definitely can't let you do that. That's a matter of safety. Any friends?" I shake my head. I mean, yes, I have friends. If I called them, someone would probably come get me. It's a matter of principle that I don't want to. I don't expect Hayes to understand. I want to disappear. No one knows what has happened except for Jon. And he's probably at the police station by now. I curl my legs further under myself and sigh.

"I'm sure there's some dark corner you can hide me in. I may be plus-size, but I assure you, I don't take up that much space." At the mention of my size, I gauge his reaction. I've never been bothered by my own weight or shape. Jon has made off-handed remarks here and there, but to hell with what he thinks. I know that my outfit today would garner nasty remarks from his family. And maybe that's why I wore it. But here in front of the hulking DHS agent? I feel fine. I feel—what's the phrase? Like a small girl.

Walking next to him in the hall, standing just beside him in the interrogation room? He loomed over me like a bear over his prey. And the way my body heated up in that close proximity? I think I wanted to be caught and eaten. I may still.

I look over to the door. There's a scanner on the outside. Maybe he's the only one with access. Maybe we can...my thoughts drift off into dangerously spicy territory for someone who only just broke up with their boyfriend. He gets up from behind his desk and comes to stand in front of me.

"Stand up." Without waiting for a response, he pulls me up by my hands. I hop to my feet, and here we are again—barely chest to chest. My flimsy Vans toe to toe with his work boots. My tight workout leggings to his cargo pants. There's something laughable about this pairing. How did my morning go from standing in line wishing I was going anywhere but Dallas to being detained and holed up in a handsome DHS agent's office?

"First of all, I don't care if you're the size of one of your cats, Millicent-Rose. I can't let you *live* in the airport for a week. What do you think would happen if you got caught and someone found out I knew your plans from the start?"

His hands once again find their way to my upper arms, and he gently grasps them, holding me down as if I'll run away. Doesn't he know he's holding all of the cards here? I know he's not stupid enough to think I'm in charge. But there's a charge in the air that tells me something is at play between us, in our dynamic.

And it's more than just agent and detainee.

"Second of all?" I hesitantly ask, on a breath.

"I have half a mind to…" His hands go to his hips as his eyes move around my face.

"To… to what?"

He shakes his head. "It just feels like…" He looks down at me, his eyebrows pinching together as he thinks about his next words. "I can't tell if you're trying to make yourself smaller, to be less perceived. Or if you truly just need to disappear for a while, and I'm half-tempted to give you what you need."

To give me what I need? Well. That could be taken a lot of different ways. I need another coffee. A better one. Not the swill they brought me. I need a nap. And I really need an orgasm that I don't give myself with three different toys.

I try to take a step back, but his hands on my arms keep me in his grasp. The confusion is written clear across my face. I know it is. Because I don't do half expressions. When I think something, it shows right up on my round face.

"No." He drops his hands. "That's not what I meant."

"Well, what do you expect me to think?" I laugh. "You said you're tempted to give me what I *need* in that gravelly tone of yours, and I just—" I fling my hands around in the air haphazardly. "My brain reacted." I pull my lips in, biting down on them to hold back a smile. "If that's not what you meant, and you're not going to let me stay in the airport rent-free for a week, then what is your suggestion?"

He brings a hand up to pinch the bridge of his nose. "I have a cabin. It's remote. In the woods. It's about an hour away." And, *no*. But also. *Maybe?* I ponder it briefly, despite red flags going off in my mind with the words *cabin*, *woods*, and *remote*. Add those together and you get me featured on a *Dateline* special on TV. *She just really wanted peace and quiet, guys.*

So, yes. Despite my logical self telling me to decline his offer, I find myself asking, "And you're just going to let me stay there by myself? With no catch?" There has to be a catch. The red flags are flying. Maybe he's planning on kidnapping me. Or worse.

"Catch? No. Well. No..." He trails off. "It's my house. You'd be staying at my house with me. But I will be at work most of the time. And I'd leave you alone. You can have the bedroom. Bruno and I will just mind our business. It sounds like you need a break. And the cabin is the perfect spot. I thought about finding you a hotel room. I'm not sure you can afford that though—"

"Wait!" I hold up my hand, stopping him from his word vomit. "You don't know me. I could be an ax murderer. I could get off on...I don't know, killing DHS agents in their remote cabins and stealing their really cute dogs."

"You said you teach second grade. Do you moonlight as an ax murderer?" He chuckles and takes up a stance leaning against his desk. When I don't respond, he continues. "Yeah, I didn't think so, Mills."

"So, what? I'm just supposed to sit there all day until you're off work? I know this guy" —I gesture to Bruno—"has to get back out there at some point. It's not a one-and-done type of situation. All the other dogs are gonna start asking where their leader is." Hayes shakes his head and snaps his fingers to get Bruno's attention.

"Let's go find Jenna and tell her we're taking a personal day." I start to follow him out of the room. "No, you should stay here. Jenna is already going to give me hell for this. I never take time off. And—" He cuts himself off, looking torn. And what? What was he about to tell me? "And just, I'll be right back, okay?" I want to argue, but I throw myself back on the couch, regardless of my mixed emotions.

"Don't take too long."

"Yes, ma'am." He leaves me in his office.

agent and my sidekick. Half my point has already been made.

"Seriously?" I point to the mess she's made on the floor in my absence. Various items from my desktop lie there in a pile. Pencils, pens. Scissors. My keyboard? "What were you doing?"

"You left me here for over an hour, and I have to pee! I tried banging on the door, but..." She throws her hands up in the air dramatically before pointing to the mess she's made.

"Oh shit..." It leaves my mouth, and I immediately hate myself. I left her here and completely forgot to have someone check on her.

"Yeah, oh shit. Now, can I go pee? Or do I need to say please? Where's the closest bathroom up here?" She shimmies around as if she's seconds away from having an accident. It's hard to control my laughter. But I do.

"Take a left, and then it's at the end of the hall. Millie, I'm so sorry. I really am. It wasn't intentional. I just was trying to get out of here, and it—*Shit.*"

She's out of the room before I can explain myself further, which is fine. I need to gather my belongings and make sure to leave detailed notes for the rest of the team under Jenna's watch today. Jenna may not be me, but she can take over while I'm out.

I know I said I would come to work this week while Millicent is at my house. Yet... she's only in the bathroom, and I'm already aching for her to come back. And the last hour, all I could think about was getting everything done so I could get her in my truck and away from all this noise.

***

This is unusual. That's the easiest way to put it.

There's a woman in my house. Down the hall. *Naked*. Using my shower. And I'm glued to my spot in the living room. The door is closed. But I can see steam billowing out. It's taking all of my self-control not to march down there and stand outside the door to ensure she's fine.Br uno nudges his nose into my cargo pants. The first thing Millicent asked to do when we got here was shower.

But I'm still fully clothed from work and unsure what to do now. My schedule is all screwed up. The sun is still out. It's hardly lunchtime.

"What is it, boy?" I bend down to scratch at his head, and he looks off down the hall. Yeah, Millie's presence is throwing us both off. We've lived here by ourselves for a few years now. Once my kid moved out, I sold the house and moved permanently into the cabin. It has suited my needs just fine. Bruno and I don't need much. We don't want much. Until today.

"She's safe, Bruno. You know that. Do you want to go check on her? Go on. No one's stopping you." I give him the gesture to run off, and he does. He's one hell of a guard dog. I knew it the moment I got him. He's got an instinct other dogs in the unit don't have. It's what makes us a great team. I watch him walk to the bathroom door and sit in front of it, at the ready, wet nose barely touching the door as he whines a little bit. Then he lifts a paw and scratches at the door. "Buddy, no."

Before I can stop him, he does it again and the door opens. Millie stands there with a towel wrapped around her body. *Barely.* The fluffy towels I keep in the bathroom for guests do little to cover her luscious thighs and breasts as she bends over to check on Bruno. I step back into my open bedroom doorway, out of sight, and hold my breath. *Speaking of hiding in dark corners.* I'm not sure what will happen if she comes looking for me right now.

"Hey, little guy. Where's your daddy?"

Fuck. The way she says "daddy" has my dick standing at attention. I run my hand down the front of my pants to quell the urge to take her just as Bruno appears in front of me... followed by Millie.

"Oh!" she shrieks, seeing my hand on my crotch. "I thought—You were—And the dog—"

"It's not—" *It's not what it looks like.* But it is, isn't it? I get one look of her naked body, standing in *my* house, and my dick has plans of his own. "It's been a few minutes. I—" I reach onto the dresser by my door and grab the old sweatshirt and sweatpants to give her. I hate that we couldn't get her suitcase. But since she didn't want to go home today, this is the best I can give her. "I have this for you...if you want them."

She reaches out, one hand wrapped around the top of the towel, and takes the clothes. When her hand grazes mine, I shudder. How am I supposed to spend a week with her in my space if a simple graze of her fingertips sends me over the edge?

"Thanks," she adds with a smile. "I'll be right out. Sorry if I used all of your hot water. That's just the best water pressure I've had in ages." She does look more relaxed than she did half an hour ago. But she's also retreating as though she's done something wrong. I reach out a hand to stall her. Any reason to touch her still-damp skin.

"I'm glad you enjoyed yourself." I'm a little too glad. If I let myself, I'll go back to thinking of her soaping up her body in the small shower stall. So I divert. "I'm going to make sure the bed is ready for you."

"The bed?" She looks past me. "It's already too much that you are letting me stay here. I'll take the couch, Hayes." I told her she had to call me by my first name if she was going to stay with me. "You and Bruno take the bed."

I shake my head emphatically. Ain't no way that'll happen. I've got a beautiful woman in my house. She'll take the bed. Sure, yeah, the couch wasn't made for my 6'5" frame, and Bruno'll have to sleep on the floor, but he won't mind. He looks up at me. Who am I kidding? He'll find his way to her side in the middle of the night.

"It's my house. My rules. You take the bed. I don't want to hear any more about it." My voice grows stern, and I stand a little taller. She pulls the clothes to her chest, bites down on her lip, and then smiles.

"Yes, sir."

And yeah, that's it. Any shred of dignity I have left is on the floor. I'm at full-mast now. And there's no hiding it. "Millie, baby, I need you to go get dressed. And, for the love of god. You can't—" I run my hand down my face, stepping further into my room.

"I can't do what?" She takes a step towards me, batting her thick eyelashes over her gorgeous green eyes.

"You've had a long day." I hold out my hand to stop her from progressing. "We—we can't."

"I can do whatever the hell I want. And from the looks of it, you want to do exactly what I've been thinking about since you patted me down this morning at the airport. I'm just not afraid to admit it. And that's what makes us different." She drops her towel and the clothes to the floor, steps over them, and walks the rest of the way towards me. "Stop refusing to admit you want your hands on my body. I'm giving consent this time. Take it."

11
Millie

What am I doing? Oh hell. I know exactly what I'm doing. I'm free for the first time in years. And this man is standing in front of me, in his house, in the middle of the woods. My mind should be screaming at me to take it easy and stay on alert. I only told Jon it was over a couple of hours ago. But Hayes has been nothing but kind and gentle all day—even when he started frisking me.

My mind and pussy are at war with what we're doing. And one is currently winning. This connection to Hayes? Even when we argue? Hell, especially when we go back and forth. It gives me a spark I've been missing for years. It's as if he wants me to fight back. To bark. Maybe even bite. It's... I feel safe. And my body craves more of that. More of him. More in general. I need him. And he clearly needs… something.

Am I delusional in thinking that something could be me? With the way his eyes are tracking up my naked body right now, I dare say not.

I found Bruno at the bathroom door whining, thinking maybe something was wrong. And yeah. Something was wrong. His daddy had a real *bone* he needed help getting rid of. It's the only thing standing between us in the semi-darkened room right now. With his back to the window, I can only make out his rising shoulders and ragged breaths. With the blinds open, I'm the one on display here. I'm comfortable with my body, even if Jon never told me how much he liked it.

I don't need a PhD to know that the way the man in front of me is reacting means there's something here he likes. I take that and let it bolster more confidence. I let it carry me the short distance to him, meeting him toe to toe. He's still clothed. Despite the layers between us, I can feel the heat emanating from him. A manly heat I need to wrap around me immediately, to infiltrate me in every way possible.

"Hayes…" I whimper. It's not a sound I'm familiar with, and it makes me nearly jump from my own skin, goosebumps rising on my naked flesh.

"Hmmm…" He licks his bottom lip before grazing it with his teeth, his eyes not leaving mine. I rise on my toes and place my hands on his shoulders. As my hard nipples brush against the soft cotton of his t-shirt, it sends a zap straight to my core, and I rub my thighs together. I've been wet since this morning. I'm half-ashamed that all it took was for him to grab hold of my arms in such close proximity, jolting me from my immediate need to run out of that interrogation room. But by the looks of it, he's not unbothered by the movement. He tilts his head back as my abdomen grazes his shaft, and I gasp as he tilts his groin into me, hard ridge meeting my soft, naked folds.

"Kiss me," I demand. I'm not walking out of this room and putting on clothes. Not yet. I knew this might be a possibility the moment we decided I would come here. We've both been in relationships in the past. I'm not naive. I know what I want.

"Mill..." At this moment, I don't mind the nicknames he's already giving me. I'm dead. "When I kiss you..." *Thank god he didn't say if.* "I'm not going to take it easy." *Please don't,* my pussy cries. "I may have been hesitant and bumbling all fucking day with you. I was only trying to hold back. I wanted to drag you into my office and bend you over my desk. But if you give yourself to me right now, that's it. I'll drain every last damn drop of pleasure from your body, and remind you what a real man is."

Fuck. Yes, please. I want that.

I slowly nod. "Yes, sir." Why aren't his hands already on me? I'm a split second from asking him this question when he surprises me.

"Fuck it—" he growls, hauling me to him with one hand thrown under my ass and the other behind my neck. Our mouths meet in a tangle of lips, teeth, and tongues. As his hand slides from the base of my neck to my throat, he pushes me away, my needy lips searching the air for his. "On my bed now. Lay back." But then, to the dog, he says, "Go to the couch." Bruno scurries off with that one command. And just like that sweet puppy, I don't need to be told twice.

But also... *I've never been the best at following rules to a T.* I back up onto the end of the bed, not getting on the bed to do as he says. Part of me wants to know if spanking is his thing. If I don't listen, what will he do? He mentioned bending me over his desk earlier. This is a man who seems to get off on being in control. I sit and wait, watching as he unzips his pants, pulls off his shirt, and then shucks off his pants and socks. Stalking towards me in just his boxer briefs, Hayes runs a hand over his cropped hair. I let my eyes wander over his body some more, making a display of admiring every available inch of skin.

"Are you testing me?"

"Yes, sir." I may bend the rules, but I don't lie.

"Listen..." He crowds into my space, spreading my legs with his wide body. Bulky. Comforting. Muscles hidden under a layer of insulation. The epitome of a "dad-bod" that I can't wait to explore fully with my hands. And my mouth.

For now, it's me who's exposed to him completely. The cool air of the room sends a chill straight through me as I'm exposed to his eyes. He runs a hand from the curve of my neck to my breast, stopping to tweak my nipple, then continues on his path down the curves of my round stomach. He keeps going, still further, his middle finger idling, teasingly hovering above my slit. His other hand finds its way to my throat again, and he pushes me back onto the bed.

"I'm waiting..." I bite down on my bottom lip and lift my hips off the bed, begging for friction. His finger slips past my folds and just barely inside me. We both inhale sharply.

"And you'll keep waiting until I say otherwise." But as he speaks, he inserts another finger, sliding them in and out of my pussy, creating enough tension to break me if he wants. I'm just on the precipice of falling. And he knows it. I can just tell this is a man who knows how to get what he wants. Despite his earlier mistakes, by the way he is scissoring his fingers in and out of me right now, I know I'm in good hands. And if he's offering me his home to stay holed up here for several days? Who am I to say no? Especially if it comes with a side of no-strings-attached benefits.

"As it is, I'm inclined to flip you over and take what I want. Bury your face into the quilt so you'll stop talking and just let me have my way with you."

"Fuck. Yes, please," I moan, attempting to sit up and roll over.

But a hand on my breast stops me. He squeezes forcefully, then removes his hand, only to slap where his hand just left. This forcefulness is *hot*. How is this real?

Did I actually get on the plane this morning? Did we crash? Is this actually heaven? A heaven where all of my sexual dreams come true, and I get a dog? I mean, I miss my cats. But at least this pussy is getting attention.

"You're weeping for me, gorgeous." He pulls his fingers out, brings them to his mouth, and hungrily sucks them to the knuckle. "Taste what you're making for me." In a split second, his fingers are in my mouth, and I'm sucking just as feverishly, only I wish it was his throbbing cock.

"Mmm..." I pull his fingers from my mouth. "I want to taste you."

"Only good girls get to taste. I'm not sure you've been good. Or did you forget how we met?"

This is all so dirty it should be comical. It's like a porno come to life and I'm the star. What have I done recently to deserve this?

"Did I forget how we met? You mean this morning? When you arrested me? Yeah. So what? I've been the opposite of good. But it's been a long, hard day." I emphasize each word with a pout. "And I need a treat."

When I go to sit on my knees, he doesn't stop me. When I run a hand from his chest, down his soft stomach, to the waistband of his boxer briefs, he only breathes harder. And then I reach my hand inside to find his swollen cock standing at the ready. He hisses as my hand makes contact, and I relish in the feel of the velvety skin under my fingertips.

"Baby…" His hands find their way to my still-damp hair and tug gently so that I have to look up at him.

"Looks like I'm not the only one weeping." I swipe my thumb over his head, gathering the drops of pre-cum there. Pulling my hand to my mouth, I suck the tip of my finger into my mouth with a wicked smirk. "Yum."

Without pause, I fall to the bed on my stomach, pull him completely free, expose him to the cool air, and wrap my lips around him with a groan.

12

Hayes

Millie's mouth is around my dick. I met her less than five hours ago. In the airport security line. Because I detained her. And now? Her fucking perfect lips are sucking on my goddamn cock, and I'm enjoying every second of it.

My hands are still threaded through her hair, and it's taking all of my self-control not to grasp harder and thrust my hips, giving her all of me—making her take me into the back of her throat. I'm not small. But Millie is taking me like a champ.

"Fuck, Millie. Yes."

The moans coming from her are about to send me over the edge. I yank her off of me and look down to find a feral, smirking Millie biting her lip as she looks up at me.

"Who are you?" I bring my hand around to her cheek and lean in to kiss her again.

That first kiss mere moments before? It was only a tease. I need more before I'm inside the warm, wet heat of her cunt. Her lips part to meet mine, and I immediately suck her bottom lip into my mouth before sweeping my tongue in, not asking for access.

"Do you always play with your food before you eat it?" She giggles, leaning into my touch.

Speaking of eating. The small taste of her wasn't enough.

"Millie, baby. Do you not know what foreplay is?"

"Obviously, I know what it is..." The way her tone drops has me questioning whether that's true. I'm worried I'm about to be offended *for* her.

"You're not a virgin, right?" Surely, she's not. But I'm not going to assume anything and risk hurting her if this is her first time. Physically or emotionally.

That has her busting into a fit of laughter. "Honey, the only thing virgin about me is my ass."

Shit. Well, there goes my last thread of willpower.

"It's just..." She pauses, rising up on her elbows. Her breasts move with the action, and I lean down and take one rosy nipple into my mouth, sucking hard, not giving her a second to finish her thought. She falls back to the bed, and her hands are in my hair again. "Fuck, Hayes. I'm trying to tell you something!"

She laughs as I move on to the other nipple, grabbing onto it and shoving it in my mouth. I look up at her and raise a brow, wordlessly asking her if she wants me to stop.

She only pulls me in closer and smiles. "Jon always just took what he wanted and left me to pleasure myself. So I'm a little..."

If she mentions his name one more time while I'm trying, and dying, to get inside of her, we're gonna have a problem.

"A little what?" I let go of her nipple with a gentle kiss to the top of her breast before leaning over her again.

"I'm having some trouble understanding. Like, maybe you're just prolonging it to stop it—I know you're older than me. I don't know how much older. But you keep treating me..."

Another kiss, this one searing. I take hold of her face, not stopping to gently do anything. I grasp and pull her towards me, crashing her into my chest, and our mouths meet again.

"You want to know how old I am? You want to know my middle name? My birthday? The names of my parents? What my fucking hobbies are? I'll tell you. But first?" Kiss. "Spread. Your. Legs."

I kiss her one more time, helping her to lie back on the bed. "I don't play. I'd never lead you on with the intention of just stopping. You think I enjoy blue balls? Shit, baby. I plan on devouring you as much as possible as long as you're in my house."

I wait until she's comfortable before crawling up the bed and laying on my stomach, wrapping my arms around her thighs and resting my hands just above her mound. "The only thing I'm interested in prolonging is your pleasure."

13

Millie

He dips his face down between my legs, and I die. With his fingers, he spreads my lips. With his tongue, he gives me one swipe from my entrance to my clit. It's warm and electrifying, and it's all I can do to stay on the bed.

When one hand finds its way from around my body and into my channel, I scream. No man has ever gone down on me with such ferocity. I should feel filthy.

And I do... In the best way possible.

My toes curl as he flexes his fingers and maneuvers his tongue, licking and sucking his way around. I don't even care how he got this good. I just care that I'm benefiting from it. With the way my body is reacting, I'm about to explode.

In what feels like a matter of seconds, an orgasm wracks my body; my legs leave the bed and find purchase on Hayes's back, and I arch my back off the bed with a guttural scream.

But he doesn't stop until I'm coming again.

Surely this isn't possible. I haven't disassociated yet. I haven't gotten my vibrator and sat here by myself thinking of all the things I wish someone would do to me. This has to be a fluke. Yet another reason I'm sure this is just the afterlife.

"Hayes... I think..." My brain is mush. This is clearly a new level of orgasm because I've lost the ability to think clearly. He must take pity on me because the pressure eases, and he slowly climbs up my body, holding himself up above me.

He lifts my leg slightly before scooting in a bit more and reaching over me to his bedside table. I follow his movements, not quite sure what he's doing. Opening a drawer, he pulls out a small box, empties it on the bed, and unwraps a condom.

I was about to let this man raw-dog me. And I somehow find myself uncaring and unashamed of the fact.

"Had to make sure you were good and wet for me. Are you ready? You can still say no." He slides the condom on.

"If you don't fuck me right now, I sw—"

Suddenly, he's pushing himself inside of me. To the hilt. And I'm frozen. Stretched. Laid out on his bed. Unable to move. Yet, I am unable to understand why he's not moving either, as he remains motionless above me.

"Did I hurt you?"

"If I die like this, that's fine. I don't care who knows."

He chuckles before starting to gently thrust inside me. "Noted. Although, I have no intention of having you die on my watch."

Only la petite mort, I hope.

"I need you to come on my cock, baby."

Trust me. I want to.

"You need a lot for a man wh—" He takes hold of my chin with his hand and leans over my body, pausing in his thrusting motion.

"If the next words out of your pretty little mouth aren't 'yes' and 'sir,' just don't say anything." I nod, his hand moves down to the curve of my neck, and he goes back to moving his hips. "Now. Be a good girl for me and come when. I. Say. Come." He exerts energy with each word, pushing in but pulling out in the same breath.

"Which is it?" *Come or come when he says?* My body doesn't know which direction to follow, with his hand on my throat, his cock in my pussy, and his words penetrating my ears. All of my senses are flooded, and I'm in heaven. My sass isn't appreciated, though. He quickly withdraws, and I yelp.

"Turn around. On your hands and knees." He helps me flip over onto my stomach and rise to my knees. Before I can fall to my elbows, his hand lands on my ass, and it sends me falling to the mattress.

"Ouch!" It stings. In a good way. My hips are pulled into the air, and he's back deep inside of me, hitting my innermost walls, parts of myself I've never even touched.

I have to turn my face to speak to him. From the corner of my vision, he's holding back on finishing. "Is this supposed to be a punishment? The spanking? You being rough? It's not a punishment at all..."

I want to see what'll happen if he lets loose. "You've got me here, show me what you've really got, Agent Hayes..." I push my ass up and into his groin. "Show me who's in control."

"Fucking hell, Mills." Hayes crashes over me and lands with his arms on either side, pressing down on my back as he comes down. With him seated inside of me and molded against me, I feel full and safe.

"Try me. Try me and see what happens." His thrusts slow down, impossibly so. "Want to see me fill this pussy?" he questions, running one of his hands down the length of my back just like he did earlier when he shouldn't have been touching me.

Now, without clothes between us, I'm about to explode with lust. I'm seconds from telling him just that when his other hand reaches down below my waist and finds my clit, giving me the tension I'm craving for a release.

At this rate, with him still thrusting inside of me slowly, and now rubbing circles over my sensitive bundle of nerves, I won't last long. This is the edging session from hell. Is this how they torture prisoners?

"I'm so close, Hayes. Please—please, I need to come!" I'm on the edge of what is already feeling amazing and I want him to finish me. Pushing my ass against him, I beg for more. "I'll be a good girl, Hayes. Let me come…"

"You think you've been a good girl?" The pressure grows in my lower stomach as he alternates rubbing my clit slowly, then quickly, and thrusting inside of me at the same time. "You've done nothing but sass me since the moment I met you, honey. I'm glad I've got you alone now and we've got this whole ice-breaker out of the way. I can have you on your knees with my cock shutting you up the next time you want to sass me."

My smile gives way to my enjoyment. "Again, you underestimate my needs and how far I'm willing to go to get what I want. You threatening me with a good time isn't much of a threat at all…" I want to feel his wrath. "Bring it."

"You asked for it." He's off of me again in one swift motion, walking to his dresser to pull something out of one of his drawers. I roll back over to see him holding up a plain black tie.

"What are you going to do with that?" I have an idea. But it's a toss-up.

"Well, I wasn't sure. But you seem to want to test me." He whips the tie around in the air and slaps it down on the bed. "I could tie your hands. But I like the feeling of them running along every surface of my body." I squirm the closer he gets to me.

"And?" I urge him to continue.

"And, your eyes are too beautiful to cover up. I need you looking at me as I take you. But that damn mouth, baby. That mouth, I think I'd like to give it something to bite down on. Is that okay? Do you think you can handle me wrapping this around your mouth?" He asks so nicely, it's hard to remember that he's about to literally gag me.

The consent is top-notch. *10/10, would recommend. Will return for more of whatever this is.*

All I can do is nod my head, which isn't enough for him.

"Words, Mills. Before I put this on, we have to discuss limits. You won't be able to talk. So, slap your leg three times. Understand?" He gently wraps the tie around my neck, taking both ends in his hands.

"Yes. I want this."

He smiles, and I open my mouth for him to gag me. But he surprises me by grabbing the nape of my neck and leaning in to kiss me first.

"Are you ready for a little *funishment*, honey?" he asks, licking the seam of my lips before dipping his tongue into my mouth. As soon as he's kissed me, he's wrapping the tie around my mouth and tying it in the back, being careful to not pull my hair. When he steps back to admire his work, that smirk on display, I can only rub my legs together. "Don't worry. I want this as much as you do. I want to enjoy watching you squirm just a little bit more..."

Stalking towards me, he opens my legs and climbs back on the bed. "Show me what I want, and I'll give you what you need."

My legs fall to either side, exposing me to his hungry stare. I can't take the waiting game any longer. And I don't have to. He throws my legs over his shoulders and pushes his way in. "Come on Mills, let's finish together. I'm almost there."

He's not lying. In less than a minute, he's folding over me with a low groan that I feel in my core. And then he's back on his stomach in front of me with his lips attached to my clit, sucking and inserting two fingers, working me up to another orgasm that wrecks its way through my body.

Only I can't shout his name. It's dampened by his wide black tie gagging my ability to talk.

And I think I like it.

14

Hayes

The sun has set, and she's lying beside me in bed, sound asleep. Her light snores fill the space, and I'm left to my own thoughts. What I felt while we fucked was nothing short of magical.

I'm not sure I can even describe it. Or if I tried to explain it to her she wouldn't run away from me.

I told her she can stay here all week. And I'm ready to offer her no-strings sex. The only problem is that I feel a definite string attached between us. Even as she lays on her stomach with her bare back exposed to me, freckles dotted over soft curves, I'm pulled to her.

And yet...

Bruno's bark in the living room has me jumping to my feet in an instant. Then, the sound of an opening door, followed by keys jingling and a familiar voice, has me reaching for pants and rushing out of the room. I close the door and rush into the living room to find someone I wasn't expecting.

"Hey, Bruno." My daughter stands by the dog, petting him on the head. She turns to see me in my cargo pants, shirtless and bedraggled with a sleepy expression, hand in my hair.

"It's Monday." We speak at the same time.

"Yeah, and what are you doing home so early?" Carly sets the grocery bags down on my small kitchen table and begins unloading them into the fridge and cabinets while Bruno leaps off the couch and follows me into the kitchen space. I reach into the fridge behind my daughter and pull out a bottle of water.

This isn't the best timing. I'm not sure how I forgot that Carly would show up. I could have texted her and told her to skip coming over this week. But I wasn't exactly thinking earlier with my right head. As I take a look around the kitchen, I'm glad she's here. What would I have fed Millie? Stale chips and canned soup? Carly is my lifesaver. I rely too much on her.

She's finishing her master's degree online in IT, and she cleans houses on the side for extra income. She manages to fit me in on Mondays, and I pay her well for it. On top of that, she does my grocery shopping. Am I capable? Yeah. I am. But she got tired of me eating takeout, cans of soup, and stale chips. Enter my kid and meal planning.

"Dad. Are you feeling okay? Why'd you come home from work early? Normally, you'd just be pulling up in an hour or so." She walks over to me and holds a hand up to my forehead, frowning. "No fever. But if you don't feel well, lie down. I've got to put all of this away and there are a few things I need to get in the oven before I get started on the bathroom."

She looks just like her mom did at this age. At twenty-two, she's tall and lanky but with muscle from years of playing volleyball in school. She's not quite as tall as me, as I'm 6'5", but she's only shorter by a few inches.

"You can just leave everything here, honey. I'll get it all taken care of. I think I will take a few days off. And I want to clean up the place on my own. I'll still pay you, though. I hate that I forgot to cancel." I lean against the counter and fold my arms. She doesn't like this answer.

"Dad."

"Carly," I return in the same serious tone.

"What's going on?"

"Nothing." I stand up straight and walk into the living room, avoiding her gaze. We've been on our own for so long; there's not much I can hide from her. Carly's perceptive brown eyes bore into my soul right now. They mimic the same brown eyes I used to look into before her mother passed away all those years ago.

As if the universe is against me, my bedroom door opens, and Carly's head turns a hair faster than mine.

"Dad!" she screams.

"Hayes!" Millie darts back into my bedroom. I'm not even sure if she was fully clothed. I wasn't standing where I could see her.

"Shit," I growl. "You." I point to my daughter. "Keep putting groceries away. I'll be—I'll be right back."

I run to my bedroom and open the door to find Millie scrambling to cover herself with the sweatpants and sweatshirt I'd given her earlier. "Baby, it's okay."

"Baby? You're going to 'baby' me when there's another woman in your house? I saw her with groceries. Did you invite me here as some sick game?" She's disheveled from sleep. Her chocolate brown hair is wild from sex. I reach out a hand to pull her in, using the neck of the sweatshirt before wrapping an arm around her waist and holding her there as she continues to fight me. She swats at me. "Get off of me!"

"Hey!" I whisper. "That's not just some woman. That's my daughter, Carly. I forgot what day it was and should have canceled with her. She comes once a week to clean and leave groceries." At that, she stills a smidge in my grasp but doesn't relent completely, pushing back on my hold.

"I walked out there in nothing but one of your t-shirts!" She is mortified. Her cheeks have reddened, and I can't help but lift my free hand to rub at them briefly before dipping my head down to capture her lips.

"Baby, she's pretty accepting. Non-judgmental. All that. If you don't want to meet her, that's fine. I already told her to leave. But..."

"But what?" She hesitates and backs out of my arms.

I drop my arm and let her, even though that pull I feel between us has me stumbling towards her as she sits down on the edge of my bed.

She looks at me for a moment and then gestures behind her. "Poor planning, my guy. Poor planning."

"Yeah," I concede. "What can I do to make it up to you?" I fall to my knees on the floor and place my hands on her thighs. She doesn't spread her legs. Good for her—make me work for her forgiveness.

"I'm starving."

I smile. "She's got food. And she's a great cook."

"I'm guessing if she has to feed you, you can't cook for yourself?"

Ouch. "No, I can," I counter.

"Yeah, okay." She deadpans. "Can I freshen up a bit, and then I'll come meet her?"

"Wait." I stand up and crowd her on the bed, wrapping my arms around her shoulders as she places her hands on my hips. I need to put a shirt on. Her cool fingers graze the skin there, and I'm only a few seconds from stripping us both naked again.

The only thing stopping me is knowing that my daughter is absolutely standing outside of the door listening in to this conversation. She comes by her nosiness honestly.

"Take as long as you need." I lean down and kiss the top of her head, grab a shirt out of my dresser, and get ready to face Carly's line of questions.

15

Millie

With the way Hayes jumped back when he opened his bedroom door, I'm pretty positive that either Bruno or his daughter was waiting on the other side. I laugh at the thought, trying to think back throughout the day. Had he even mentioned kids? Or did we jump straight from the interrogation room into each other's throats and pants?

He did say he'd give me all of the answers I wanted. I guess this answers one of them. His age? Old enough to have an adult daughter. Hopefully, she's not as old as me. Because well... I'm not ready for that talk with her or my parents.

When I asked if I could freshen up, I'm not sure what I meant. I don't have my toiletries. Or any other clothes, until my suitcase comes back from Dallas. So I simply throw my hair into a messy bun and run a hand down the front of this ill-fitting ensemble. The pants are a little too loose in the waist and a little too long in the legs. And the sweatshirt's sleeves need to be rolled up a bit. Beyond that, there's no helping *this*

I take a deep breath before calmly walking into the hallway and out into the open space of the cabin's living room and kitchen. Three heads turn to look at me from their places by the kitchen counter.

"Hi." I wave awkwardly at the new face and take a moment to really take her in.

She's almost as tall as her dad. Whereas he has light brown hair that is cropped and graying at the sides, her dirty blonde hair is long and straight. She smiles and elbows Hayes, who elbows her back in return. I wonder if she favors her mother. Because watching them side by side, I don't entirely see the resemblance.

He sees me watching them closely and waves me over. "Carly, this is Millicent. Millicent, this is my daughter Carly."

We shake hands before I'm pulled back by Hayes into his side. I'm not prepared for him to wrap an arm around my shoulder like we're long-time lovers or boyfriend and girlfriend. I'm merely an orphaned traveler staying at his house who saw an opportunity to bang her savior.

I look up at him with confused eyes, furrowed brows, and my mouth ajar. He lifts his index finger to my chin and pushes up, closing my mouth.

"You'll catch flies, Mills."

"Mills?" I say just as Carly chokes on whatever it is she's drinking. Calling me Mills in private is one thing. But to call me that in front of his daughter gives her the idea that we're something more than security officer-and-detainee with benefits.

"Well then. How long has this been going on? How'd you meet? I have so many questions. I've never met any of my dad's girlfriends."

I don't have time to even shake my head before Hayes speaks for me. "Oh, you know. It's still new. But exciting. And–" It's my turn to elbow the man. "*Oomph.*" He tightens his grip on my shoulder, pulling me in closer. "It's—"

"We met today, Carly," I say, completely in opposition to whatever narrative Hayes was trying to put together. Carly's mouth falls open as her brown eyes widen, and she doubles over in laughter.

"Oh my gosh, Dad. This is... This is..." She can't catch her breath between laughs, as she pulls out her phone and begins typing. "Happy to know I'm not the only whore in the family."

"Hey!" her dad shouts, his free arm swinging out as if to grab the phone she's pulled from her pocket. He misses, and she turns slightly to avoid another attempt.

"I'm obviously talking about you, Hayes Oliver Collins. Gee whiz. You think I'd stoop so low as to slut-shame a woman the first time I meet her? Or ever?" She's typing away but lifts her gaze to me once again. "Millicent, Mills, what do I call you?"

"Millicent or Millie is fine," I smile through the embarrassment of whatever is happening here. I may be boiling alive on the inside, but I still have my manners. "Do you want any help with the food?"

I look behind Carly to the counter, where several bags are open. Quite a bit of produce and meat haven't been put away yet. I need to do something with my hands to distract me from this, whatever *this* is.

But the younger woman shakes her head, hands on her hips. She's wearing athletic shorts that show off toned and tan legs with an over-sized, old high school volleyball shirt.

"Oh, no. No. You're my dad's guest. I'm going to plug my headphones in and get to work. Are you staying for dinner?" She's already turned and is setting aside a container of raw chicken, a package of cheese, some tomatoes, some bread crumbs, and a box of pasta. "I'm making chicken parmigiana and a salad."

"Um—" I start before Hayes interrupts.

"Yeah, she'll be here for dinner. If you're sure you're fine, honey, I'm going to go talk to Millie outside." He reaches into the fridge and grabs me a bottle of water before grabbing my hand and walking us to the front door. I slide on my Vans from earlier and follow him outside.

All we can hear are the sounds of the bugs as they serenade us from beyond the porch steps. Without the sounds of traffic, they're almost deafening. There's no light pollution up here. No next-door neighbors. This is one of the strangest predicaments I've found myself in as of late. But I'd take the constant yapping of the cicadas over Jon's mother's incessant negative comments about my body and my personality—anything about me, really.

I stride over to one of the rocking chairs on the small porch and settle down, not entirely sure if he meant for us to talk here or away from the house. When he joins me in the other chair, though, I know I've made the right decision.

"A whore, huh?" I joke. "It seems like you guys have a pretty solid relationship."

"Yeah." He smiles. The light from the kitchen window illuminates his face. "I'm still sorry that I didn't call her."

"Hayes. She's your daughter. I'm a random woman you met this morning at the airport. I know which one of us takes precedence." It hurts a little to say because we may have only just met, but I'm too comfortable sitting on his front porch, wearing his clothes, talking to his daughter, and about to eat his groceries. *Not to mention riding his cock a few hours ago.* In the whole scheme of things, the latter is probably the most important one.

"Yeah. A random woman," he echoes, a look of complete seriousness overtaking the smile he wore only seconds ago. His gaze drifts from me, moving off the porch and into the vast darkness beyond the house.

"This is peaceful. Doesn't it get lonely, though?" The questions I want to ask are at the back of my tongue, raring to jump out. I'm not sure either of us are ready for those. Even though he told me he was an open book in so many words, I'm not sure he understands the gravity of that.

"Lonely? No. I prefer it up here. When..." He stops and leans forward in the rocking chair. It creaks with the shift of his weight. I'm in no hurry to push him. "My wife passed away ten years ago. I had our house outside the city up 'til a couple of years ago. But...it was filled with too many memories. And..."

Again, I'm not sure if it's the right move, but I stand and move to sit in his lap. Who knows if this damn chair will hold us both? I don't care at this particular moment. I have the urge to be impossibly close to him.

Snuggling into his side, I speak just above a whisper. "I'm sure nothing will ever be as lonely as losing a spouse, a partner, the mother of your kids."

Though he let me slide into his lap and he's cradling my waist with his arm, the change in his demeanor is noticeable.

"Hey," I whisper, pulling his face toward me with my finger under his chin. "I'm sorry."

Two words. I never met the woman, but if Hayes loved her, she couldn't have been half bad. And if Carly looks anything like her, well, she was a gorgeous woman.

He leans into my shoulder and stays there momentarily before I hear him mumbling underneath his breath.

"What's that?"

He sits up and licks his lips. "I said…" He takes a deep breath before pulling me in for a quick yet searing kiss. "We might have only met this morning, but I hope you'll stick around for a lot longer than a week."

If I weren't sitting securely in his lap, I'd fall to the porch.

"Hayes…" I'm flattered for sure. But I'm floundering for what to say. "We slept together once!" I lower my voice to a whisper.

Carly is cooking on the other side of this wall. Headphones or not, I'm not taking any chances. When I start pulling away to stand up, I'm yanked back to his chest, his arm wrapping around my shoulders, and he lowers his lips to my ear.

"Don't tell me you don't feel whatever this magnetic pull is between us, Millie baby." His hand drifts from my shoulder, over my breast, and to my belly, where he lets it rest dangerously close to the elastic waistband of the pants I'm squeezed into.

"It's called lust, Agent Collins." I mean to sound strong, but it comes out in a husky whisper.

His pinky dips beneath the elastic now, and he wiggles it back and forth until he can slide another finger in, brushing against the skin of my lower stomach. It may be lust, whatever I'm feeling, but the truth is that I've never felt so desired. No crumbs here. And while it is a welcome feeling, it's also scary. I'm unsure that I can trust it.

"Call it whatever you want. I've got you right where I want you. You said you wanted to disappear for the week. And I'm here to make sure that happens. You want to fuck all over my house? Done. Want to take the truck up to the top of the mountain and just lay in the grass by yourself? Be my guest. But do it with me here. And know that you're not getting rid of me anytime soon."

"Hay-Hayes…" His name falls from my mouth as he slides the rest of his hand in and finds that I'm not wearing any underwear. "Are you about to…" I can't even say the words.

His freaking daughter is just on the other side of the wall, and he's got his large hand down the front of my pants, millimeters from grazing my clit. Two of his fingers spread me apart while another enters me just barely. What I learned earlier is that he enjoys the tease, the buildup, making me hot for his touch.

"You don't think I can't get one out of you before she comes out here looking for us? Besides, I've already been called a whore tonight. Better to just live up to the name." He chuckles into my neck, warm air fanning over the exposed skin there.

I don't doubt he can. I doubt that we won't get caught with our hands in the proverbial cookie jar. Because that's where my hand is sliding now: over his and into my own pants.

Send me straight to hell. If this isn't heaven, that's where I'm going. I'm about to let this man get me off on his front porch in the middle of nowhere while his daughter cooks us dinner inside. What's one more embarrassment to add to today's tally?

16

Hayes

I 've said very little about this to anyone before. My late wife knew about my desires to dominate. She encouraged it. When I lost her, it nearly took me too. But Carly needed a parent, and I had to keep going.

Meeting Millie and having her test me today? It's caused this dominant side of me to resurface. That long-dormant part of me who craves control like this. Of a woman. Of having her be putty in my hands while I strum her clit with one hand and hold her against me with the other.

"You think you can be quiet about it? You think you can stop yourself from squealing like you did earlier while I have my fingers in your pussy?" I ask, letting her push my hand further into her pants. She's a brat through and through. She's testing my willpower.

If Carly weren't here, I'd have this woman on her knees and begging for me to stop giving her pleasure. As it stands, I'm only seconds away from doing just that when she starts bucking into my hand. "Baby, you're so responsive to me," I coo into her ear, letting her do most of the work as she continues riding my fingers

Later, when we're alone, I'm going to revisit the comment she made earlier about her virgin ass. If that's the truth, I'm going to have too much fun introducing her to that side of life. If she wants to leave after her week here, by all means.

But it won't be without my cum leaking from all three of her holes.

"You're so close, aren't you? Use me. Take what you want. I'm here to give you exactly what you need, remember?" *A place to stay. A shoulder to lean on. But especially fingers to come on.*

"Hayes..." She whimpers quietly, her hands going to the armrests of the chair, grasping. "How is it that you can get me there so f-fast... my body... it never does this..."

She's squirming uncontrollably against me. Her lips are on mine, and she's straddling my legs in the chair. If we aren't careful, we're gonna cause a scene that'll surely bring my kid and dog out here.

There's no way to hide this *if* Carly opens that door and steps outside. It's now or never.

"Come on my fingers, baby. Come for Daddy." The words are out of my mouth, and she's flying off my lap, my hand jerking from her pants suddenly.

"What—"

"Why'd you stop?" I try to maneuver my hand around to the front of her pants to get back inside where I really want to be. To the warm heat of her pink cunt.

I have no neighbors. Tomorrow night, I'm bringing her out here and stripping her naked to eat her out in this same spot. Just the thought has me salivating.

I lick at my lips while letting my eyes roam over the curves of her body hidden by my sweatshirt and pants. "You were so close. I know you were. I felt it. You didn't want to come?"

"Oh no. I was. I do." She crawls back onto my lap and leans in, gently licking the corner of my mouth. "Just... Daddy, huh? I think I like that." She grinds her hips into me. "You prefer that over Agent? Want me to call you 'Daddy'?"

I am impossibly hard, ready to explode if she doesn't stop.

"Millie..." My hands drift to the sides of her face, and I cradle her there for a moment, pushing her away as she pushes in, creating tension. If I take this inside, rushing us to my room, my daughter will know what we're doing. And I can't take her here on the porch with Carly here.

But—*My truck.*

I stand up, and she falls off my lap, but not to her ass because I've ducked under her arm and thrown her over my shoulder all in one move. With another one of her adorable squeals, she smacks my ass. I swat at hers in return.

"Where are you taking me?"

"We're gonna defile my truck before dinner."

17
Millie

*D*addy.

I've never had a daddy kink. Until this very mo-ment. Until the moment this man had his fingers buried in my pussy and told me to come.

Maybe that was just the code to activate the sleeper cell slut inside of me. And if that's the case, sign me up for a lifetime in his service.

He opens the passenger door to his old truck and pushes me up into the seat before rounding to the other side. When he shuts the door, there's no pausing. He's immediately on me, pushing me against the door, hands in my hair, and his knees in the seat. Neither of us are small. He's what I'd call burly. Stocky. I'm not sure how this is going to work out.

There's no time to question whatever his process may be, though, because my pants are coming off, and his cock is springing free from his cargo pants. He squeezes himself between my legs, placing one of his knees on the floorboard as well as one of my feet. We're inches away from connecting again, and I want it so bad.

"We don't have a condom." He stops before the tip is at my entrance. "*Shit*."

"It's okay," I tell him. "I'm on birth control. I need you, now." He looks at me tentatively, and I nod, reassuring him I mean it. "Take what you want, Hayes. Fill me with your cum."

"Fuck," he growls, and follows it with a moan, notching himself inside of me and sliding all the way in. There's a clear difference in the feeling of him without the extra barrier of protection and I'm not taking that for granted. He glides up to the hilt and stops, arching his back. "I don't know if I can—*fuck*, Millie. You feel so good. I don't know how long I'm going to last. You sure you want me to finish inside of you?"

I nod again.

This man has a breeding kink. I could smell it a mile away. I may never have experienced it with someone, but I've read enough smutty romance books to spot it. At least, I'm pretty sure.

"Daddy wants to fill me with his cock, doesn't he? Wants to know I'm dripping with his cum while we eat dinner later?" I reach my hands up to his shoulders and gently scratch down the front of his t-shirt-covered chest, wanting to rip the whole thing off.

"Gah..." He pulls out and then pushes back in slowly one time before pistoning his hips in a quick rhythm, giving us the release we both need. "Honey, you have no idea..."

His hand drops to my entrance, wetting his fingers. Then he brings it to my clit, working it in slow circles before dropping it down below to my asshole, sliding a now lubed finger around the tight ring. "When we're alone again, we're gonna talk about me taking you here."

I gasp in surprise, the words stuttering out on a moan. "Oh, god..."

The feeling of an orgasm is working down my spine, up my legs, meeting at my core as I clench down on him. He stalls in his movements and groans, his eyes rolling back in his head.

"Take whatever you want, Hayes!" I come with a shout and he follows suit, both of us a panting mess in the cab of his truck. I don't fucking care. He can have whatever part of me he craves.

"Don't tell me that if you don't mean it." He hovers over me and smirks. "Because I'm not sure I can let you go after that. I'm claiming bits and pieces of you and..." He bites down on his bottom lip and leans down to kiss me. "Just..."

His finger slides into that previously untouched orifice of my body, working in tandem with his tongue as I part my lips for his greedy exploration. He's not finishing his thoughts, leaving me hanging here half-dressed and half-understanding what's happening.

It's true, though, the parts I understand of what he's able to say. He's claiming bits and pieces of me. Parts I've kept hidden away and guarded from others. But Hayes comes in and wrecks that whole wall in less than twelve hours.

Maybe he's right. Maybe there's been an invisible string, a magnet of sorts, between us, and we only just got through the knots today, drawing us to one another.

"If you're serious about taking the week... I'll stay here, and we can see where this goes. But I..." I hesitate.

Hayes's lips capture my gasp as he pulls his finger from my hole. Pulling away, he smiles down at me. "Whatever you want. We can discuss it after Carly leaves. But we should clean up and get back inside because dinner's probably about done."

He sits up and pulls me with him, handing me my pants from off the floorboard where he threw them. With a gentle hand on an ankle, he guides one foot into the leg of the pants and then the other and helps me pull them up. When his hands reach my waist, Hayes doesn't stop there, pulling himself up into the seat next to me and pulling me into his side with an arm around my shoulders once again.

This is too comfortable. I'd live here if allowed. It *shouldn't* be allowed. Because it shouldn't feel this real and this good all at the same time. I take a deep breath, all at once overcome by these new feelings and the fact that he is very much dripping from me, and I'm going to have to make it into the house and change into a different pair of pants without his daughter finding out what we've just done.

"What's going on in your head?" His hand drifts over my shoulder and brushes a stray hair behind my ear as he reclines in the bench seat. *A lot and nothing*, I'm thinking. But I don't tell him that. I only smile and lay my head on his shoulder.

When I do go to speak, a bright light from the porch catches our attention. Carly has stepped out the front door, one hand on her hip, the other raised above her eyes. She's looking for us.

"Dad?" We're not too far away to hear her shout into the dark.

"Watch this," Hayes whispers, leaning over to the steering wheel. With the click of a lever, he's blinding her with his headlights, and she's jumping back a few feet with a shriek.

18

Hayes

"I love you. And she seems great. But sitting with the both of you at dinner? That was…" Carly mimes an explosion with her hands from her head. "Too much. I have to go." She throws an arm around me before scratching Bruno behind his ears.

"I don't know how to explain it," I begin.

Millie excused herself to give us a moment alone and I'm wishing she were here right about now. Not as a human shield, more just as the warm presence I've already grown used to. Yeah, I had a hand on her the entire time we ate dinner. And possibly my eyes were on her the whole time, too… Most definitely my eyes. Who would blame me? The woman is effortlessly gorgeous. Or maybe I'm just entranced.

She sat at my small table in my sweatshirt and another pair of my sweatpants and ate chicken parmigiana with me and my daughter like this wasn't the first time she'd met either of us. And as soon as my daughter drives off down the dirt road? I'm marching down the hallway to claim that woman again in any way she'll let me.

My eyes drift down the hall to where my mind already is, and Carly follows my line of vision.

"Dad, ew. Just go. I swear." With a punch to my arm, she squeezes past me and lets herself out. "Use protection!" she shouts, and I shudder. I never thought I'd be subjected to this particular treatment from my kid. There's a reason she's never met any of the women I've dated or slept with.

So, I have to think there's a reason everything worked out the way it did: how I forgot to call Carly, that Millie agreed to come home with me, that we seem to fit together like she's the missing piece to the hole in my heart. No one will ever be able to replace my late wife.

And that's a conversation I've had over and over again with my daughter. It's a conversation I had to have with my wife when she was on the brink of death so many times—when the doctors would give her only weeks, and somehow we'd squeeze a few extra months until the days just ran out. How I've managed to raise a functional human being without her is beyond me.

And yet, I'm standing here in the cabin I live in to escape from the world, contemplating being with another woman and having more kids at forty-five years old. I've lost my mind. That's the only explanation. I've lost my goddamn mind.

Before I race down the hall, dick out, I run my hand down my face and try to hold myself back. One week or one day, whether she knows it or not, I'm not sure if we're getting out of this as two separate people.

"You coming?" Millie shouts from the bedroom, and my feet start carrying me towards her siren call, even if my brain is stuck in the what-ifs of what we are doing. Of what this could be. Of what it isn't. She pops her head out from behind the door and smiles. But when her eyes land on me, she frowns. "Everything okay?"

I pause and nod. "Of course. Carly left. I just…"

She meets me in the middle of the hall, and I wrap my hands around the back of her neck, pushing back her hair so that my fingers meet her warm skin, intertwining there and pulling her forward to kiss her forehead.

"We've been sort of busy with other things; we haven't had a chance to talk."

"Is that something you want to do?" she asks, wrapping her own arms around my middle and hugging me. "I mean…This can be…That is to say…I don't expect anything out of this. I already feel like I'm using you for a place to stay, and then we've had sex and…"

"Hey," I command on a breath, squeezing her tighter. "It takes two to tango." She laughs at my lame joke, and I fall just a little harder. And then, our moment is interrupted by a phone ringing in the bedroom—an unfamiliar tone. It must be hers. She lets go and runs after it with a huff.

19

Millie

*O*ops, *I Did It Again* blares from the bedroom.

That ringtone only means one thing: my sister is calling me. I didn't check in with her when I landed in Dallas. Because I didn't land in Dallas. And now I'm about to pay for my stupidity.

"Livvvy," I elongate the hard *v* sound in her nickname. "Sorry I didn't check in."

"Huh. And why is that? Is it because you didn't even go to Texas?" I can picture her tilting her head with a raise of her brow, questioning my answer. We're only two years apart in age, closer to that in the way we look. If I can imagine myself making a face, chances are it's because I've already seen her do it.

"What do you mean?"

"Knock it off, Mill, you know I follow you on Find-MyFriend. Your location is on. And your cats and I are five minutes from jumping in the car to come and find you unless you tell me what's going on. Why does it say you're in the mountains? What happened? Where's Jon?"

I feel a warm presence behind me and settle into Hayes's chest as he wraps his arms around my soft middle.

"It's sort of a funny story. I didn't get on the plane."

I pause to let her gather her thoughts.

"Okay. But that tells me nothing. You never wanted to go on that trip to begin with—Jon was making you. And I don't hear yelling, so I can only assume he's not with you. Unless," She gasps. "Did you do it? Did you finally break and murder him and drive west to dump his body at a pig farm? Oh, Millicent-Rose. I'm so proud of you, honey."

My younger sister squeals into the phone while I sigh at her antics.

"No. Last I checked, he was alive. It's a long story. I can explain later. But..." I tilt my head to the side and up to find Hayes's eyes. He smiles. "I broke up with Jon this morning. And a friend offered me their cabin for the week."

"What friend do you have that owns a cabin?" She presses. She's not going to let this go.

"Hold on," I tell her and then put myself on mute. I turn to Hayes. "She's not going to stop asking, and she'll only keep calling me. If I don't answer, I assure you, she already has your location. So I'm going to turn on the video chat option."

I won't if he says no. Or if he doesn't want to be on the screen, he can leave the room. But this is his home. I'm just his guest. That's all. But when he takes the phone from my hands and switches to video himself, I'm left shocked.

"Hayes!" I whisper-shout just as my younger sister's face fills the screen.

"Millicent-Rose, tell me right now, where the—Fuck! Who are you? Where's my sister?" Olivia's eyes are wide as they move side to side, taking in everything about the man behind the camera. He's holding the phone just far enough out in front of him that I'm able to slide under his arms and stand in front of his chest.

"Liv, I'm fine." I tilt my head up and roll my eyes at Hayes. "This big guy is just trying to be funny. He's not going to hurt me."

"Well, that doesn't explain who *this guy* is, Mills. I don't hear from you all day, and then you show up at some random man's cabin? Looking..." My sister pauses to take inventory of my face. "You look different."

Of course, she'd immediately clock the *difference* in my demeanor. Besides the obvious difference being the tall, stocky man standing guard behind me, I'm wearing his clothes and a permanent grin from our day's activities. I'm 99% sure I have hickeys in places she'd blush at.

"I feel different," I respond confidently. "To answer your question, this is Hayes." I relax against said man, and he drops a hand from the phone to rest on my lower stomach. Nothing with him feels wrong. Not even when he puts his hands on my body where I'd normally cringe from my usual insecurities.

It's quite possible that all I've needed was someone to dominate me in order to give me more control over my own feelings and life. However strange that may sound, I'm willing to continue testing it out.

"Just Hayes? No last name? Is he famous? Why the secrecy? And honestly, it's unlike you to do this." Olivia's eyes keep bouncing back and forth between me and Hayes.

Hayes only squeezes me tighter against his chest before leaning down to whisper in my ear, "I'll give you a minute, baby." I know I blush at that—I can see it in the camera—but also, the heat spreading through my body at the term of endearment is a dead giveaway.

Olivia's jaw hangs open as Hayes kisses the top of my head and leaves me alone in the bedroom, closing the door as he leaves. She doesn't last two seconds before screaming, "Millie! What the hell is happening?"

I fall onto the bed and scream back, "I don't fucking know! I mean, I'm alive, right? I didn't die? Like that plane didn't fall out of the sky? You checked before calling me?"

I'm still somehow convinced that this isn't real. This shit doesn't happen in real life. It's made up in romance books written by women, for sure, but not something that

I'd ever be worthy of having happen to me "for real life," as my *Bluey-obsessed* niece says.

"Um, yeah you're alive. Speaking of which." She bends out of the frame but is back quickly, holding one of my precious babies. "Latte heard you." My tortie claws at Liv, attempting to climb onto her shoulder and get to me.

"Baby girl! Where's your sister?" I coo into the phone, and the pain of missing them hits me right in the heart. Yeah, it's barely been twenty-four hours, and I wish I had them in my arms. But if I have to choose between sleeping in Hayes's bed, wrapped in his arms, or making my way to Olivia's house and sleeping on her couch for a week with my cats—her kids jumping on top of me every waking moment?

I love my cats, but this is a no-brainer. All three pussies are getting a vacation from their normal life, either way.

"I know it's a lot to ask, Livvy…" I lie back on the bed, pursing my lips, knowing I'm about to get an earful. "I need this." Lowering my voice, I watch her slowly pick up what I'm not saying.

"You're seriously going to stay there all week? With a stranger?" She doesn't pause in her round of attack. "I get it. You broke up with that *asshat*, and the adrenaline is coursing through your veins. You did something stupid, but I can come get you now. Seriously. I have your location."

"I swear…" I have to take a deep breath and think about what I'm going to say to my sister. Because she will come and get me—it's not that far away. I know that if I walk out and tell Hayes I need to leave, he'll take my hand and walk me to his car, himself. And that's why I know I'm safe here. It's going to be hard to leave.

Olivia catches me biting down on my bottom lip and scolds me. "What're you thinking? That's your 'I'm think-ing something naughty' face."

"Oh, please." I burst out in a fit of laughter. "You don't know me." But even as I say it, I'm drifting back to *hard* thoughts of Hayes between my legs. I can't stay on the phone much longer if this continues.

"You're in trouble. Wait until I tell Mom and Dad..."

"Please don't." Here we go again. Why is it that I'm the oldest and yet the only one treated like a child? That's the last thing I need: my dad showing up here on Hayes's doorstep. The thought has me ready to bolt. I'm mostly aware that was her intention. "You can't scare me out of this. Let me be stupid for a week."

"For a week? Honey." She *tsks* me.

"I have to go," I tell her, done with this conversa-tion. Just because she's married with kids and a mortgage doesn't mean she gets to dictate what I do with my life. Without waiting for her to respond, I add in one more thing. "And please don't come looking for me. I'm fine. Hayes is safe. I'll keep my phone charged and my location on. Okay?"

Then I hang up on her and throw my phone across the bed. Hayes cracks open the door only a moment later.

He had to have been standing out there the whole time, waiting for me to finish the call. I sit up on my elbows and beckon him forward with a crook of my index finger.

"She gonna come up here and steal you away? Should we go to my next hideaway?" He crawls over me on the bed but then settles on his side with only a leg thrown over mine.

"Another hideaway? You got any more cabins out here? Or are we off to the mountain caves next? Is this the part where you tell me you're actually a serial killer on the loose?" I snuggle firmly into his side, taking in everything I can.

I want him again—I have to stop myself from climbing on top of him. After this week is over, I'm going to need to flush out my system. My body has never taken this much all at once and this many times in a row before. He shakes his head. "Sorry to say, this is it. And the only thing I'm guilty of right now is wanting to murder your ass." He licks at his lips and holds back a laugh while I let mine go.

"That was..." Oh, god. This man. "We get it, Agent Collins. You want to take my behind. You want to captain the USS Millie's Peach. You want to—"

I'm stopped by his hands on either side of my face as he roughly pulls me in to kiss him, his beard scratching at my lips and cheeks as we go for it, tasting one another, enjoying each new experience as they come to us today.

"Stop talking, and let me have this." His hand runs from my flushed face straight to my ass, where he squeezes. "It's all I've been thinking about since you walked out of that shower. Before you even told me you'd never been taken there." His hand works its way around the roundness of my ass before he settles it under the elastic of the sweatpants, working his way down into the crevice with gentle fingers. "Tell me I can have it, baby. Tell me it's mine, and I'll make sure it feels so good," he growls, one of those fingers casually slipping over my hole.

I'm caught up in his words, of how they're making me feel. Because even though he's pushing the subject, it doesn't feel *pushy*. I'm as greedy for it as he is. I'm ready to turn over on all fours and give him what he's asking for. Whoever I was when I woke up this morning flew away with the wind when I walked out of that airport. And the woman who replaced her? I like her.

"Take me, Daddy. I need you in my ass."

20

Hayes

"**F**uck, woman..." It appears that whoever I thought I was dealing with is nothing compared to this vixen. "You've had my cock in your dirty mouth. In that wet cunt..." I push my fingers into her core and feel her clench around them. "And now—" I reach over to my side table and open it, grabbing a bottle of lube and a condom. "You want Daddy to take your ass and make you completely his?"

"God, yes, please. That's all I want..." She climbs onto all fours and pushes her ass into the air. My nerves are vibrating with pure need right now to get inside her. I can't wait one more minute.

"My needy little slut won't be an ass virgin after I'm done with her." I'm up on my knees and behind her, peeling off her pants in one swift motion. She helps me by kicking them off onto the floor, and before her ass is in the air again, my face is between her legs, licking from her clit to her tight hole.

"Shit!" Millie jerks back, rams herself further into my face, and I laugh. She's only helping me more. With a loud "Yes!" she rocks back and forth. She likes this—*wants* it. That only spurs me on more to continue greedily attacking her puckered opening with my tongue.

I don't have any toys here for her. If she's going to be here longer than a week, I'll fix that. I've never overnighted a vibrator or a butt plug, but there's always time to start. For now? We've got to work with what we've got, and that's my fingers, my tongue, and my cock. All of which I'm dying to get inside of her. I crack open the lube and drizzle a good amount down her crack, eliciting a squeal.

"Shit, Hayes! Warn a girl. That's cold!"

"Sorry, baby. Just in the moment. Ready to get in here and—" I work the lube down, around, and into her hole with one of my fingers. "Take you." I pause with just my fingertips in, gauging how she's feeling.

Pushing back, she turns her head to look at what I'm doing.

"You gonna do it or tease me, big guy?"

"If you've never had anything in your ass before, baby, you need to take it slow and prep. As much as I want to ram this cock up your perfect hole... you need to have patience." I end with a laugh, gently pushing my finger in little by little.

"Well, how long 'til we get to the main attraction?" She's biting down on her lips as I twist the tip of my finger back and forth just past the surface. She moans again, and it takes everything in me to not roll her over and shove my cock in her mouth and give her something to moan around.

"When you get used to having more than just my fingertip breach your asshole, Millicent." I first-name her, flatly. "Or do you not think I'm big enough to warrant working up to that?" As I question her, I slide my finger further in, up to my second knuckle, and allow her the time to adjust. She tenses slightly under my grasp, clenching down on my finger.

"Wait..." She tenses, and I ready myself to pull out. But the question out of her mouth has me on the verge of laughter. "Is—is it too big?"

I'm not sure if she's joking. When soft green eyes meet mine, I'm thrown off.

I go to withdraw my finger, but she stops me with a hand to my wrist. "Don't you dare! Just keep going. I need you in my ass, Hayes."

Her pouty lips, her soft curves—they have me enraptured. I grab onto her side with my free hand and hold onto her soft middle, wanting nothing more than to bury myself in every square inch of her.

"I'm not sure I've ever been asked that question about anything other than a margarita on taco Tuesdays," I mumble. That's not entirely true. At all. She knows it.

"Sure..." She flips herself onto her back, dislodging my finger for a moment, and spreads her legs once again for me, "I'm sure no one has looked at that... thing"—Millie licks her lips as she admires my shaft -"and said, 'yeah, probably the smallest penis I've ever seen.'"

I've got my finger inside of her again, adding a second, bringing my free hand down to stroke myself as she watches unashamedly. Still, somehow, this isn't enough contact. I need more hands. More body parts touching her. I give up stroking myself and focus on her clit instead, rubbing rhythmic circles with the pads of my fingers as she relaxes further into the bed.

"Yeah, relax. I need you to come at least two more times before I breed your ass." I wink and keep up my twisting and rubbing until her back is arching off the bed, and she's a squirming pile of heavy breathing, loosened limbs, and cursing under her breath.

When she comes, it's with a scream and a smile on her face. "We're almost there," I tell her with a smirk, knowing exactly what I'm doing.

She wants my cock in her ass? She's going to have to work for it.

She sits up on her elbows, her brows pinched together.

"Almost? And two more times?" She whines.

I don't think I'll ever get enough of teasing this woman. "Well, one now. And then you'll thank Daddy for letting you come."

I reach for the lube and add a good amount to my fingers once again. "Let's try for a third finger, shall we? You think you can take another one of Daddy's fingers? Is your asshole getting all nice and ready for my cock? Is your needy little hole begging to be filled with my cum? Tell me what you use to make yourself come, Millie. I want to imagine you using them to get off."

I'm ready to explode just thinking about her fingering herself. Her wet pussy is dripping right now, and I want to lean in and capture it on my tongue.

"Fuck. I don't think—" She cuts herself off, her mouth shutting and her lips squeezing together as she loses her train of thought. I'm focused on working three of my fingers inside of her again, but I'm not going to ignore what just happened. She was about to open up, but something stopped her.

"You don't think what? Tell me, Mills." I look up to see her staring at the ceiling.

She shakes her head, and I can tell she's starting to pull back mentally. For as much as I don't know her, there's something about the way she's acting that I understand completely—some vulnerability that my heart is pulled to respond to and comfort. It far outweighs what my body craves right now.

"If you like what I'm doing, you'll tell me. If you don't…" And my dick doesn't like the next part, but it needs to be said. "We stop. No explanation needed."

"That's cruel," she adds, looking down her body to meet my gaze. But the next time she opens her mouth and another little breathy moan slips from her lips, I know I've got her on the hook. She likes what we're doing.

"No one has ever talked to me like this. And I think it might be an addiction." She strings her words together quickly, with no breaths in between and it has me on the verge of both laughter and tears. Because a life with no exploration of even the most basic of kinks? What kind of life is that? There'll be time to hold her and explain things to her.

Right now, though? Right now, I'm going to keep showing her what she's been missing out on.

21

Millie

His dirty talk took me out of my own head for a moment. I drifted off, left my own body, and watched us from afar. I didn't recognize myself, watching us writhe on the bed together in pleasure. And then I plummeted back into my body when I told him I was addicted to his dirty mouth. If that's not embarrassing, I don't know what is.

I lift myself up on my elbows and let my head fall back on the pillow, pushing my chest out.

"That's right, let me take care of you." He moves his free hand to my center and inserts two fingers, curling upward in a come hither motion, over and over. "I said give me one more. I know you can. You're such a good girl for Daddy."

Fuck. Is he going to ramp up on the dirty talk now that he knows I like it?

As if he's reading my mind, he laughs. "That's right. Do you hear how wet you are for me?" He works his hands in tandem. "I think you're almost ready for Daddy's big cock." He elongates the hard sound with a heavy breath. "Let me see you come first, and I'll give you what you need." He quickens his pace, curling his fingers up, in, and around, and I fall apart again.

Before I'm able to come down, my legs are bent over my own body, as he folds me in half like a fucking pretzel, and he descends on my hole with his hot tongue. He rims the outside only for a moment before adding in a sucking move that has me gripping the comforter tightly.

Testing my own bravery, I reach down and grab hold of his head, pulling his hair but pushing him further down at the same time. He hums into my ass, and I can't take it anymore—the edging has to stop.

"Now, Hayes. Fuck me now. I swear. I'll leave if you don't take me now!" I'm not sure that's the truth. But it does the trick. He's on his knees and gesturing for me to do the same.

"Knees, baby. Hands and knees. Show me that pretty hole." I follow his directions, immediately pushing my ass back out for him to take in any way he wants. I want to get to the main attraction, as I called it moments ago. "If this hurts at any point, you tell me. Pick a safe word. It can be red, but I need to know it." He caresses an ass cheek as he steadies himself behind me.

"Red. Red is fine," I say, ready to start. "I promise to tell you if it hurts. Please, Hayes." My ass meets his erection with force, and he grunts.

"I'm going as fast as I can. Trust me, baby. I want this as much as you do." I hear the crack of the lube again and am prepared this time for the cool hit of it on my skin. I barely shiver this time as he works it in with his thumb. "You'll feel a little pressure, and I need you to bear down as I'm entering. Don't forget to relax."

He keeps talking me through it, gently coaxing me like this is my first time ever having sex—and it certainly feels like it. If only my first time were half as good. It certainly didn't include a patient partner, foreplay, or time spent making sure I knew what I was getting into.

"Relax and bear down."

I inhale deeply as he notches himself at my hole. This is happening. I'm losing my anal virginity to a stranger, and it's the best I've felt in years. The most invigorated. The most in control of my own body. I don't want it to end. He slowly but surely enters, inch by inch, until he's fully seated and takes hold of my hips.

"Fuck, Hayes. Are you in all the way?" He has to be. I feel so full.

"Yeah, I'm in," he answers, not breathing.

I look over my shoulder to find him barely holding it together. His eyes are closed, his lips are pulled in tight, and his neck is strained so much, there's a vein popping out on the side. "How is it? Can I—can I move?" Even as he speaks, his hips start to thrust just slightly. My clit throbs, and I can't help but to bring my hand down to my core, rubbing myself softly as I nod my head for him to start moving, finally.

"That's right, touch yourself. I want to hear you scream my name."

"Daddy," I moan, leaning my head into the pillow and biting it as he thrusts in and out.

"Who does this hole belong to?" He doesn't wait for me to respond before wrapping a fist around my hair and yanking my head back. "That's right. Me." Leaning down closer to my ear, he nibbles at my lobe before whispering, "Don't forget that."

Who knew possessiveness in a man could be attractive? Jon could never—*fuck*, why am I thinking about Jon when this man is... *Ohhh.*

He drops his hand down and pushes my own away from my tender clit and picks up the pace of both thrusting from behind and circling his fingers right where my bundle of nerves is screaming for yet another release.

What a greedy thing that clit of mine is.

Speaking of greed, I push back harder just as he thrusts forward, a slap echoing in the space as our naked flesh meets. It's a gratifying sound—a more than pleasant feeling. I do it *again*, and he slaps my ass this time, *hard.*

"Gods, yes. Do that again, please. Harder." I can't contain the moan that slides out between my parted lips.

"I'm not surprised you like it hard." He chuckles as he takes hold of my side with a solid grip. It's a part of my body I'd normally be ashamed of. But the way he's holding it, massaging it even, it's not bothering him. It'll leave marks—ones I'll wear proudly from our little tryst. "I'm not going to last much longer, baby." He increases the pace, dropping his hand from its strokes, replacing that hand on my other side. "Can I come inside your gorgeous ass?"

"Spill wherever you want to, god. Just..." He pulls out before I finish my thought, yanks off the condom, and inserts himself within seconds. I'm full once more, and the world is righted. "Fuck, yes. It feels so good. Fuck me raw, Hayes. Fuck."

"Yes, I need you dripping with me. Fuck, Millie baby..." He grips me harder, somehow.

Once. Twice. Three pumps is all it takes, and he's falling over me, spilling inside of me. He pulls out again, though, and I have no time to think of what's next because he's on his back and under me, shuffling so that I'm squatting over his face.

"Hayes! What are you doing?" I move to get up, but his hands around my thighs pull me back down.

"I'm finishing what we started. Sit your ass down." I'm left to grip the headboard when he attacks my clit with his tongue, then a sucking force. And within seconds, I'm squirming on his face, sitting fully, and on the verge of another orgasm. My body is limp with exhaustion.

"I'm so close, so... fucking... close..." I arch my back, close my eyes, and give myself completely over to the moment.

"Let go. Give me your pleasure. I need it. I won't rest 'til I have it."

"You arrogant bastard... I can't do it again! I've already—" How am I supposed to force another orgasm out of my body?

His large hand reaches up and squeezes my neck, and I'm suddenly shaking, holding off my release to no avail. It rips through my body and I fall over, breathless, ready to admit I'm done.

I look down and see that his release has fallen from me onto his beard, and is mixed with my own wetness, next to a nearly cocky smile. He throws in a wink, and I fall apart.

"Arrogant bastard..." I exhale, using the term again.

"An arrogant bastard who just got you off a few different times. I was too busy watching your reactions to count. But next time? Next time, baby, you're keeping track."

He gently pushes out from under me and then ushers me onto my back. "Rest a minute. I'm going to grab us some water. And then we need a shower."

"And sleep, right? Do you sleep at night? It's so late. We've done nothing but fuck all day. I'm so tired!" I fall back on the pillows with a heavy sigh. "Give me water. Or a shower. I don't care. But you'll have to do the heavy lifting, I'm afraid."

22

Millie

"Your suitcase is at the airport..." Hayes stands at the stove with his phone in his hand. I can't exactly read his expression. But by the hoarse tone of his voice, he's not excited about the fact. We've had a little under eighteen hours together.

That should be enough, right?

The last several hours have been spent in bed, wrapped in each others' arms. And last night, we were intimate in ways I never could have imagined.

I should be sated.

So why is my body still pulling me towards him? And why do I want to say *fuck it* and forget everything in the suitcase?

Hayes turns to me and frowns, pocketing his phone. He's busy cooking eggs, and I'm sitting at the counter with a cup of steaming coffee that I didn't make for myself.

I'm too comfortable in this space. I already know where he keeps the mugs and the silverware. Despite my wanting to forget the outside world exists, I'm afraid if I stay any longer, I won't be able to leave. How is eighteen hours enough time to somehow fall hard for the man walking towards me with a plate filled with my breakfast? How do I explain this to everyone?

Do I even need to?

"I can hear you thinking from over there." He slides the plate in front of me, runs his hand over my back, and then sits down on the barstool beside me. "Did you hear me?"

"Yeah." I heard him, obviously.

My heart thuds dully in my chest at the thought of all of this coming to an end. As much as I questioned this reality yesterday, the impossibility of it, I'm not sure what will happen when I step out of this house. "My suitcase is at the airport. I guess we should go get it. And I should call my sister."

She'll probably need to meet me there if she can. I've lost my appetite and the eggs in front of me no longer hold the same appeal that they did when he stood in front of the stove, shirtless, cooking them for me. But I don't want to be rude. So I take a careful bite in between sips of coffee.

"We can go get it whenever you want. Jenna already pulled it. It's in my office." His hand lands on the small of my back and he rubs small circles with his thumb there. Then we settle into a silence; maybe it's comfortable on his end.

I take another bite of the perfectly cooked eggs, composing myself, my thoughts, before I say something I might regret. How do I navigate this? We said a week. But I'm being given the perfect opportunity to escape—an out. He can just drop me off at the airport, I'll grab my suitcase, and we never have to see each other again. I don't even need to fly out of Charlotte anymore in the future. I can avoid him at all costs—I'm sure of it.

His hand presses down harder on my back, migrates further up to grasp my neck, and he turns my face to him. "I asked you what you were thinking, Millie."

There's no room for interpretation in his statement. This isn't a request, it's a command. He turns in his chair and brackets me with his thick thighs, caging me in with his warm scent and bare chest.

Biting down on my bottom lip, I sigh. There's no way out of this. Either I have this conversation with him in the comfort of his home or we do it at the airport. And only one of those sounds appealing.

"I'm thinking this has been a great past day and that I'm thankful you gave a weary girl a place to stay and..." I pull my lip back in, not sure how to approach the topic. His hand drops from my neck, but it doesn't go far, landing on my thigh. "It just makes sense for you to go ahead and drop me off, and I'll have—"

"Fuck, Mills. Does this feel like I'm ready to say goodbye yet?" He grabs my hand off the counter and brings it to his crotch, where his hardened dick waits for me under his sweatpants. Just as quickly, he moves it to his bare chest, placing it above his heart.

It's difficult enough with my hand on his body. But now he wants to bring his heart into it?

Fuck, indeed.

I scrunch my hand, pulling at the smattering of hair and trying to pull away, but he holds my wrist still keeping me from taking my hand back.

"No, baby. Feel what you do to my body and heart." Under his skin, I feel the rapid beating of his heart as it clamors in his chest. "If you want to leave, I'll take you wherever the fuck you want to go. Hell..." He lifts his other hand to cup my cheek, pushing a strand of my hair out of the way. "But if you want to say goodbye today, I'm going to prolong the process. I'm going to make sure we get in a really good, really long..." He pauses and licks at his lips. "Kiss, so you remember who claimed you."

Leaning in, he lets go of my wrist, grabs hold of my face with both hands, and captures my lips. We both must taste like coffee and lust.

"I had no plans on backing out early. I'm so lost in you, it's..." His hands drift into my hair, and he pushes my head back as he peppers kisses on my cheek, my nose, then my lips. "It's infuriating. I should be at work right now. Instead, I'm at home debating whether or not I'm going to lock you in the basement." I tense, and he laughs, but his hands tighten in my hair. "There's no basement. I'd make one just to keep you here, though." His blue eyes darken, a look of pure hunger passing through them as he looks over my face and dives back in for another kiss. "But as it stands, finish your breakfast and get your shoes. I'll take you to the airport, and you can decide whether you want to continue this."

When he pulls his hands out of my hair, the loss is sickening. I want them back on my head as much as I want to escape the overwhelming presence of the tension in the room. It's so thick, I could swim in it. I find myself wanting to swim in it.

"Carly would find me," I warn him, hoping she'll be on my side if the event were to occur.

When he leans an elbow on the counter and chuckles, I know I've got him there.

"That's the other thing, Mills. She isn't nice to everyone. But you two last night gave me hope that maybe... I don't know." He scrubs at his face, letting go of whatever he'd been about to say, moving on. "My girl lost her mom at a pivotal age. It takes a long time to earn her trust. And even longer to earn mine. Yet, here we are."

He leans his head to the side, resting on his closed fist but keeping his intense stare on me. It's like every conversation we've had so far has been serious. It's a lot. And it's all hitting me now as he looks at me over a simple plate of eggs and cups of coffee.

***

Twenty minutes later, shoes on, and backpack packed, we're in Hayes's truck. Unlike last night though, Bruno sits in between us. No matter that the dog is here and it's daylight outside, I can still feel, still smell, what we did last night.

The carnal lust hangs in the air like the rays of the early morning sun. Something almost tangible, yet not. I fidget with my hands in my lap, focusing on what I need to do when I get home. *Get the cats from Olivia. Pack my boxes?*

Wait.

If I'm not staying at the apartment with Jon, should I leave the cats at Liv's and then just move the boxes into her garage?

"Ugh," The groan slips from my mouth before I stop it, and Hayes's hand is on my shoulder a second later.

"You okay? Do I need to pull over?" He's so watchful, attentive to my every need. He's too kind. And everything I've ever wanted in a partner. I'm about to walk away from him because why? Because we met yesterday and claimed every inch of each other? It doesn't make any sense.

Yeah, the logical part of my brain yells at me. *That's exactly what we're doing. No man in their right mind does this type of thing. Not only is there something wrong with him, there's something wrong with you. He doesn't want you. He just wanted a warm body. You fit the bill.*

Shit.

I lift my fingers to my mouth and start nipping at my nails on one hand, chewing around the cuticles and nail beds. It's a nasty habit I return to when stressed. A warm hand grabs my own just as the truck pulls over on the side of the highway. We aren't too far from the airport. Maybe another half hour. He really is prolonging this.

It doesn't matter that Bruno is in between us; Hayes somehow scoots closer to me and takes hold of my face. I resist turning it, but he wins, giving my chin one final tug.

"I took the rest of the week off work. And you're technically on vacation. No one expects anything of us right now. We can sit on the side of the road 'til we're blue in the face from holding our breath. Or you can talk to me," he pleads, letting go of my chin. "I loved every damn thing we did together, but my first priority is making sure you know you're cared for and safe. If you don't feel either of those things, I'll..."

"You'll what?" I test him, though I'm feeling less brave than the girl who stripped and took what she wanted yesterday. Because this feels real now. It no longer feels like I'm floating through a dreamland, needing to be pinched or woken up. I know there can only be one outcome. There has to be only one outcome. And we're just prolonging it, making the goodbye harder for ourselves.

"Honestly, Mills. If I haven't shown you the type of man I am in the last twenty-four hours, and you don't want to stick around for the rest of the week, I can't make you. I don't know how else to say that I want you to stay here with me. Possibly forever. And if that makes me crazy, then so be it."

His chest rises and falls with his heavy breathing as he cautiously places an arm on the back of the bench seat. "Because yeah, I'm crazy for you, and I want to explore that. I'm a forty-five-year-old man who knows what he wants. I don't play games."

Hayes and Bruno are too in sync. Sensing he may be in the way, Bruno sits up and climbs over Hayes's lap, giving the man even more space to work with now. Or maybe it's because the man had moved so close to me he was almost leaning over the dog. But he takes the open spot and moves in on me, wrapping his arm around my shoulders and pulling me into his side.

"I don't play games, either." But even as my words come out, they have no conviction. Hayes knows that as well as I do.

"Baby, when are you gonna learn to not lie to me?" His gaze dips to my mouth as he tilts his head and grazes my cheek with his lips, his beard scratching at me as he does. "I claimed you. You're as much a part of me now as my own fucking pulse."

"Hayes... You're... You sound..."

"What? I sound crazy? You don't think I know that? You don't think that for every thought you're having over there that this isn't real, I'm not having the same exact thoughts?" He's laughing now. He's dipped his head to the crook of my neck, and his warm breath sends a shiver down my spine, making me want to climb into his skin. But that's the hormones talking, not the rational part of my brain.

With the way he's looking at me, the way his blue eyes are heated with desire? We're about to set this truck on fire on the side of HWY 321. That'll make the news for sure.

"Neither of us are thinking straight, Hayes. I know you offered me the space. But that was before we—" Before we *fucked*. He's claimed dominion over every part of me. He says he *wants* every part of me.

Experience has taught me, though, that not all of me is worthy of such attention.

23

Hayes

When I told Millie I had nowhere else to be, I meant it. I meant that I'd prolong the process as long as possible. Her suitcase is sitting just fine and secure in my office. We can sit here on the side of the road for as long as it takes for her to be honest. I'm ready to take my heart out of my chest and hand it to her, open hands and open-ended. If that doesn't say something, I don't know what will.

I've got my nose in her neck, inhaling. She smells like my body wash, my clothes, like me. And that only heightens my need to possess her.

She says neither of us are thinking straight. This is the clearest I've thought in years. The moment she dared to brat me in my own airport? The clouds cleared in my head, and I knew I needed her. If she thinks I'm going to just let her walk away?

I have to stop a growl from escaping my throat. As it is, I'm having to hold back the part of me who wants to claim her on the side of the road.

"Um, Hayes…" Millie gently pokes at my chest. I look up but leave my head on her shoulder.

"Yeah? You ready to tell me what's going on in your beautiful head?"

"Ha!" She chuckles. "No. Just wondering if you're really turned on right now or if you…" She trails off as both of us peer down at my crotch, where my dick is uncomfortably very much not resting behind my zipper.

"Ah, yeah, no. I started thinking about last night in the truck… and how I'd like to do it again… But—" I'm cut off when she slaps at my chest.

"Not happening, sir." Giggling, she kisses the side of my face before pushing me away. "We can't sit here all day. I'd like my suitcase. And—We need to…"

"Yeah, I know." I don't need to be reminded again of what we're supposed to be doing—that we're on the way to the airport.

Yesterday, I didn't know this woman. And today, she's sitting in my truck, holding a piece of my heart. Hell, a piece of my soul, if I'm being honest with myself. The only thing I can do right now if she wants to keep me away is to shut it down and close off my emotions, not let her see how she's affecting me.

I've played my cards. It's in her hands now—my heart. The ball's in her court. I'm so far gone, I've resorted to using cliches. She owns me. So I shoo Bruno back to the middle seat and put the truck back into drive. For the next forty-five minutes, we drive in silence, only listening to the sounds of the radio as it plays in the background.

***

"Hey, boss!" Jenna sees us enter the upstairs hall and waves me down as she exits my office. I coolly smile and gesture for Millie to walk to my office ahead of me.

"You remember where it is? If not, Bruno can show you the way." I wink as Bruno trails behind Millie. Millie rolls her eyes at me.

"Yes, sir. We were just here." When she walks past Jenna with a small wave of her hand, Jenna smiles back. But when my office door shuts, Jenna turns around and shoves me into the empty viewing room.

"Spill." My agent and friend leans her back against the door, blocking me from leaving.

"Spill what, Jenna? We came to get her suitcase. If you'd let me leave now, we can be on our way, and I can finish what's left of this spur-of-the-moment vacation…"

"Yeah, see, that's the thing. You *never* take a vacation, let alone days off. If there's someone out, you're here. If there's a holiday, you cover so someone doesn't have to. We love you for it. So when you said you needed the week off, we were all more than happy to cover for you. But now? I'm asking for payment in the form of details." She sticks her hand out in front of her and curls her fingers inward.

"Pay up."

"You're relentless. It doesn't matter anyway. It was risky taking her home. I shouldn't have."

"Don't you mean it was *frisky* to take her home?" Jenna clearly thinks she's hilarious as she wiggles her groomed brows at me suggestively. When I don't laugh, she continues. "You knew I was relentless when you hired me. I was very clear in our interview." She doesn't take her hand down, because she's not easily intimidated—by anyone.

And in this small space with me standing so close to her, my arms stretched over my chest, my brow furrowed, and my lips curved in a scowl? It's not affecting her at all. She respects me as her boss and as a person, but there's nothing I can do at this moment to change her mind. When she wants something, she goes after it like a bloodhound on a scent trail. Or like Bruno when he wants a piece of bacon on a lazy Saturday morning.

Needless to say, I'm not getting out of here without giving her something to chew on.

"Jenna..." I uncross my arms and lean against the one-way mirror, crossing my legs at my feet. "I—"

Where the hell am I going with this?

"Spit it out, Hayes," Jenna grumbles, urging me on with her hands.

"Do you believe in love at first sight?"

"Do I—" Her mouth is open, her jaw moving, but no words are coming out as she tilts her head to the side, then to the other. "Are you telling me that you love..."

She wipes her hand across her mouth. "Do you love her? Boss..."

"I know." We're both shaking our heads. Her at me. Me, also at myself, in disbelief that I'm asking her this question. I'm not even sure I know who I am. "She wants to leave, I think. I know. I feel it. She wouldn't talk to me most of the way here."

Jenna shakes her head. "I don't know. Did you trip and hit your head? Did you take something? Do you have a fever?"

"Or..." I start to say, biting down on one corner of my bottom lip. "I'm being given a second chance at love. At life. And fate just has a funny way of intervening."

Jenna backs away from the door and opens it, letting me leave.

"Well then, why are you asking me my opinion? If you want her and you think she even feels a little bit the same, go tell her, you idiot."

As I hurry out of the room, Jenna slaps my back and then she's running in the opposite direction, laughing hysterically. That woman. Honestly, I'm happy for the break for a few days. But now that I'm headed back to my office, there's a growing knot in my stomach. Something feels off.

It's not until I open the door and see Bruno, but otherwise find my office empty of a curvy brunette and her suitcase, that I realize just how right I was to worry about the gut feeling.

24
Millie

Honestly, he left me here with my suitcase and walked off with Jenna. What did he expect? For me to wait for him? Probably, yes.

I look at Bruno. "That's exactly what he expected." But I don't have the nerve to do this the right way. I need to make a clean break.

Without pause, I grab my suitcase by the handle, open the door to check that the coast is clear, make my way down the hallway, and back out the way we came. Two agents are walking in just as I walk up. Neither of them stops me.

I guess it's true what they say, if you look like you know what you're doing, no one will question you. Even if you're a civilian walking out of a classified area of the airport in the middle of the day.

I'm not taking my chances and asking for their permission. I need to get to the taxi line and haul ass out of here. I'm almost to the escalators and to the lower level when a rough, calloused hand grabs hold of my wrist and pulls me backward.

"Ma'am, you need to come with me."

"I'm sorry, what?" I try to yank my arm back, but it's no use. Hayes is standing beside me with a scowl and his trusty companion at his side. Bruno even looks pissed somehow that I am running away. Because I am. There's no past tense—this is still happening.

He won't let me go so I gesture with my head to a set of rocking chairs by the baggage claim area. He reluctantly agrees and ushers me over, but not before taking hold of my damn suitcase.

"I don't know if you know this, Agent Collins, but as of yesterday morning, I was free to go."

We both settle down into the white chairs as hundreds of people mill about. It's hard to think that no one is eavesdropping on our conversation. But damn, if they are, I couldn't care less. I need him to say what he needs to say and let me leave.

"Don't 'Agent Collins' me, Millie. I've had my cum inside you. You know my name," he says flatly. But then leans in a little closer. "We sat on my porch last night, and

I had you falling apart on my fingers, on a rocking chair just like this one…"

Like the smart-ass he is, he runs his hands over the armrests of the chair with a wicked grin. I feel my cheeks heating under his gaze and the intense memory of last night. I can't let that sway me from what I need to do.

"I think it's best if we just say goodbye here." I go to stand but he puts his arm out, stopping me.

"And I think it's time we talk. If you're not going to tell me your feelings, then at least let me be serious about mine." He pauses, like he expects me to argue with him. As if he didn't spill his heart in the truck on the way here. How could he have more to say?

I'm about to argue, though. Because what feelings? The feelings of lust and infatuation? That's what I've narrowed mine down to. They aren't something I have time for. It's time to figure out life on my own.

But he quickly adds to his last statement. "I'm not just talking about the sex, Millie…" His eyes roam the length of my body. How in the hell he finds me attractive right now, sitting here in a pair of his old sweatpants and a sweatshirt, is beyond me.

"Talk then." I wave my hand and lean back into the seat. I look down to see that Bruno has already laid down at his owner's feet and closed his eyes. So I close my eyes too. Wrong decision. Strong fingers grab my cheeks and turn my face abruptly.

"Wha—" I bumble.

"This show you're putting on? It feels like a ruse for attention. And remember what I said about games? I don't play them."

He doesn't let me answer, but it doesn't matter. We both know that was meant as a rhetorical question. Slowly, he releases my face, and I relax my jaw.

"I don't know why or how. But the moment I saw you standing in line yesterday," he laughs to himself as if he can't believe what he's saying, which makes two of us. "I was drawn to you. Yeah, I could have gone about detaining you and Jon differently. I definitely shouldn't have let myself get carried away and start the pat down the way I did."

The look in his eyes is pure lust as I watch him roll his tongue around his mouth before opening his lips again to say something else. "But Millie, baby, are you going to sit there and say that you don't feel something?"

Oh, Agent Hayes. I am feeling so much right now.

I feel the need to climb into his lap and have him hold me. I feel the need to tell him that, yeah, I feel that pull to him. Like our hearts are two ends of opposite magnets, made for each other. That somehow, through space and time, we found each other. Yet, it still seems absurd. And I refuse to admit it to myself... yet.

"What if we need time away from each other?" I ask, on the verge of tears.

"Baby." The way the term of endearment falls from his lips like a prayer has me ready to fall to my own knees and worship this man. "I just found you. What we need is more time together. All I'm asking is for the rest of this week. The week that we decided on before we let feelings and our..." He pauses, biting at his lips. "Sexual chemistry, get involved."

One week could make or break me. One week could mean actually admitting everything I've tried to keep from him. It could mean letting the feelings deep under the lust and infatuation come to the surface and be present. *Can I do that?*

"We've only scratched the surface of our potential together, Mills..." Hayes scoots his chair impossibly closer to mine and rests his hand on my knee. "Please."

I'm not entirely sure if it's the look in his blue eyes—the pure, raw look of a broken man in need of a loving touch—or if it's the whispered "please" that flows from his bruised lips that turns the tide in his favor.

I lift my thumb and pull on his bottom lip, letting my hand fall through his beard and onto his chest. His heart is beating so fast. What I won't tell him is that so is mine. The longer I keep my hand there, resting against the broad plane of his chest, the more in sync our rhythms become, letting me know that my mind might be fighting this, but my heart isn't.

And maybe that's all I need to know to jump into this fully with the man in front of me. I hesitate briefly before I move to stand up.

"Well, are you coming or not? I hate airports. And if we aren't going on a trip, why the hell are we even here, Daddy?" The last word is a test, falling brattily from my tongue.

And it earns me the reaction I want. The vein in his neck pulses as he strains to contain himself. He blinks, unmoving from his chair.

"You're...coming with me? Back to the cabin?" Slowly, he stands up, unsure that I'm not joking and might run away again. He's unsteady on his feet. I'm waiting for him to tackle me.

I step around my suitcase and wrap my arms around his waist as best I can. The man is as solid as a tree trunk. I love it.

"You just spent the last ten minutes making your case. Don't get scared now because I got the nerve to say yes all of a sudden. Take me back to your cabin, Hayes." I reach up on tiptoes, needing to kiss him. He obliges, bringing his hands up to cup my cheeks with a gentle force and giving me the touch I'm craving.

"But first," I start, pulling away from the warm and fuzzy moment, "can we go get my cats?"

Epilogue

Millie- 5 months later

"Invisible String," Hayes says, curled up next to me in bed, giving me one of the most serious faces I've seen on him to date.

"You're kidding me. That's the song you're saying is *our* song? Out of all the songs in the whole universe?" We're lying naked under the covers, hands intertwined with his arm around my neck. "I never picked you as a basic white man, Hayes Oliver Collins."

"First, I'm not basic." He rolls over a little to face me a bit more. "And I think it describes us fairly well." This man. He's a girl dad if I ever saw one.

"It's a little too on the nose. And I wouldn't call you detaining me in an airport 'invisible string theory.' As fun as that was." I laugh, thinking back to five months ago when we met that fateful day at Checkpoint E and all that it eventually led to. If ever there was an award for most ridiculous meet-cute, we'd for sure win. "Not that I'm complaining."

We both won in the end. Whatever it is he was looking for, he seems to have found in me. Likewise, I'm not sure how I breathed before him. Five months ago, I'd be up and out of bed by now on a weekend morning, slinging espresso. Now, I'm laying in bed with Hayes knowing for sure this was never going to end up anywhere else than here. He releases my hand and brings his fingers up to caress my cheek.

With no makeup on and my morning hair a mess, I know I'm not a vision of beauty, but he doesn't look away. He leans in and drops his lips to my mouth, lingering there briefly, before moving to my forehead and dropping a kiss there.

"I'm gonna get coffee and breakfast going. Stay in bed as long as you want." That's not something I need to be told twice. He pulls back the covers and steps from the bed, naked. Before opening the door, he reaches for a pair of boxers. "When I open this door, they're all going to come in here, though..."

They always do. We can't keep them out even if we try.

My babies and Bruno sit outside the door all night, just waiting for us to let them in if we've decided to close it on them. Obviously, Bruno is better trained. But the cats have been a bad influence on him, no matter how trained he is. As soon as he whips the bedroom door open, Latte and

Orca zip into the room and onto the bed, pouncing onto my feet with loud *meows*. It doesn't take long for them to work their way up the blanket to my awaiting arms.

Bruno sits just outside the door, in a guarded stance. Since the day I moved in, he's always watched out for me, never having to be told what to do or when to do it. The amount of safety and organization in this house from that man and his canine is still mind-blowing.

Hayes is back in less than a minute, sans breakfast, and even more depressing, without coffee. Bruno is behind him, though, with something in his mouth. My boyfriend pats the bed and gestures for the dog to climb up and sit next to me.

"Give it to her, Bruno, just like I said." He drops it gently by my hand and I smile. No breakfast or coffee. But an early-morning present? It's not our six-month anniversary yet...I'm not sure what else it could be. I got a key to the cabin the week I moved in—the week after we met.

"I'm a little worried now. And confused." I pick up the box and bring it to my chest. I'm stark naked under the covers. The blanket is pulled so far up it's almost to my chin. Hayes likes to keep his house cold. I think it's because it gives me more reason to cuddle with him. Although, I know it's because he just runs hot. I'm only prolonging this now. The box is in my hands and I'm looking at him as he watches me with a smirk.

"Baby, just open the box. It won't bite."

"I don't like surprises." I throw it back at him. He chuckles, picking it up and handing it to me, leaving one hand covering the box while his other sandwiches my own from underneath.

"And you don't think I know that? Honey, I know you like the palm of my own hand. Like each crevice, where each scar came from. Yeah, I just got the book five months ago, but I studied extra hard. And I'm ready to take the test."

The test?

With his hand leveraging mine, he cracks the box open, not removing his eyes from my unblinking ones. When his eyes shift down, I follow.

"Hayes! *Holy shit*! What the *fuck!*"

The words leave my mouth before I think better of it. Because what's in front of me isn't a key to a house, or a car, or anything of that nature.A simple yet stunning princess-cut diamond sits atop a thin gold band. He smiles at my outburst and keeps his hand on top of my own. My eyes bounce back and forth between the gorgeous ring and the man in front of me.

When I've regained my composure, he's down on both knees, resting his elbows on the edge of the bed.

"Are you asking me to marry you right now? We're both practically naked and in bed on a Saturday morning!" Honestly, this man could have asked me to marry him four months ago. I was that gone for him already. I'd have screamed yes so loud it'd have caused a rock slide. But now, he smirks, and I know I'm in trouble.

Standing up, he quickly shucks his boxers once again and then joins me in the bed, jumping onto his spot beside me and scaring the cats away. They scurry back down the blanket and onto the floor.

"No, now we're both naked. And the sooner you say yes, the sooner I can make love to my fiancée." He's hard already. That's not something I'd easily miss.

"We just had sex." I scoot a little back from him with a sigh. I'm only feigning annoyance, and he knows it. He may have gotten me, but I still play hard to get.

"Yeah, that was when we were boyfriend and girlfriend. Say yes, and it'll be a whole new experience." His eyebrows dance as he licks his lips, his arms coming to wrap around my shoulder and waist. "If it's the ring, if you don't like it…" He reaches up to take it from my hand. "I'll get you a different one." There's a hint of sadness in his voice even though he's offering me the world on a silver platter.

"Hey!" I snatch it back, closing my fingers back around the ring in its box. "Don't you dare. I'd love it even if you proposed to me with your so-called invisible string, you big loon." I open the box one more time and take the ring from the cushion before handing it to him, pinched between my thumb and pointer finger.

"Hayes Oliver Collins, make me your wife." Sliding out from under the blanket, I throw one leg over his middle and straddle him. "Put the beautiful ring on my damn finger and fuck me, please."

"Fuck? Not make love?" Hayes slides the ring onto my left ring finger, which I've offered to him.

"The two are interconnected where we're concerned, honey." Once the ring is on, I slide my hands up and around his neck and situate myself over his hardened cock, sliding gently over him, back and forth, coating him with our combined wetness. His hands fall to my hips, and he pushes me down harder with a groan.

"Now get on this cock and ride your fiancé."

Before his lips reach my own, I pull away. "I don't think you've asked me." I bite down on my bottom lip with a laugh. I literally just begged him to marry me. The joke is on me.

In seconds, I'm on my back, and he's inside of me, thrusting slowly as he lifts my legs up to his shoulders. Slipping his thumb inside my mouth, I bite down, and he moans.

"Millie-Rose, baby. Marry me." He pulls out with the statement, then he slowly pushes back in. "Is that better? Is that what you wanted? Or would you rather I get on my knees in front of you and beg for your hand? Hm?"

He pulls out again but settles near the foot of the bed, and the empty aching of my pussy is soon filled with his tongue.

It was never a question whether I'd say yes *when* he asked me to marry him—I've been waiting for the moment. If he held off any longer, I'd have jumped him myself and popped the question with a blade of grass from the front yard while we sat in the rocking chair sipping coffee.

"Yes." I widen my legs, greedy for more of him. "Yes, I'll marry you. Soon, please. As soon as possible!" I'm careening over the edge, an orgasm ripping its way out of me with Hayes's name on my tongue.

"How soon?" All of a sudden, he's resting both hands on either side of my face, careful not to pull my hair that's fanned out over my pillow.

"Can't we just bask in the moment?" I smile, knowing we can't. Especially now that I've put a timeline on things with my desire to hurry. If he wanted to go to the courthouse today, I'd be hard-pressed to say no. Luckily, it's a Saturday. Then I remember him telling me that Jenna got ordained once to do her cousin's wedding.

I freeze.

"Four months," I barter, biting down playfully on my bottom lip.

He dips down and kisses the edge of my jaw. "Two." As he moves along my face, kissing the corner of my lips, my nose, my cheeks, I squirm.

I counter, wrapping my legs around his waist, and pull him down on top of me. "Three and a half."

"Okay, from my point of view, it looks like you can be negotiated with, baby." He may be forty-five years old, but he does this thing sometimes, especially when he's excited.

His shoulders do a slight shimmy, and his blue eyes shine brighter. This is what I'm looking at as I respond.

"Oh." I chuckle with a grin. "I'm up for a negotiation. Want to hear my terms? You get to marry me in two months. I don't even need anything big. We can do it here with just Carly, a few friends, and some family. And I get—"

"Fuck it. You can have whatever you want." My full thought isn't out before he's offering me whatever it is I'm about to say. "Name it. It's yours."

He's on his hands again, pushing himself up onto his knees. I unwrap my legs and follow him so that we're face-to-face, sitting up in our bed.

Time for a serious conversation, I guess. He licks at his lips, watching me, waiting to see what my offer is—what I want in return for a quick wedding. Taking hold of his broad shoulders, I grab him and straddle him, lining us up perfectly. Slowly, I sink down.

"I want you to make good on your promise and start putting babies inside of me as soon as we say *I do*."

Continue Reading

Want more Hayes and Millie? Click here for a bonus epilogue.

And continue reading here for a sneak peek at book 2 in the Flight Crew Series, titled Delayed Arrival.

Sneak Peek

I'm so excited to share a snippet from book 2, which is already well under way. Please know, however, that parts of this are subject to change, as this is still a draft.

TEN YEARS AGO

Grace

The fanfare of graduation isn't lost on me. This is an exciting day—I can't lie and say it's not. I've spent the last four years working towards this goal and it's finally here. I'm free of this place—free of homework and all-nighters and answering to professors and chapel days.

But as I follow Sam, his lithe hand wrapped around mine and tugging me through the crowds, I keep my head down. I'm overwhelmed, to say the least. About to curl up in a ball, to say the most. This is another one of life's precipices that I'm not ready to leap from just yet. The emotions of the day, mixed with the knot forming in my stomach, have me about to pull to a stop. This knot is telling me to trust my gut, that I know what might happen as he tugs me closer and leads us over to our families.

Ring by spring.

That's an actual phrase. I've seen it happen time and time again in the four years that I've been a student here. Every year at graduation, at least one guy gets on one knee and proposes to the love of his life, but it's hard to not let my mind wander to what their futures look like. What mine will look like. If what is happening is what I think is happening.

Both my racing heart and mind inundate my ability to make sense of it all. That knot grows larger, forcing what little breakfast I ate to the top of my stomach and further.

"Guys! Hey!" Sam calls everyone around. We've stopped under a big oak tree situated in the middle of campus and the great lawn.

"Thanks so much for joining us today at graduation. I don't know about Grace, but I'm so excited to be done. I've got some time left to work on my flight hours, and Grace will start job hunting, but before we head out to lunch, I had something else I wanted to do..."

He hesitates. I loosen my sweaty palm from his hand and run it down the front of my black graduation gown. I'm wearing a sleeveless white sundress underneath. My mom said it wasn't dressy enough, hence why I haven't taken this polyester monstrosity off yet. But I'm sweltering, even with the forgiving shade of the large oak's branches above us.

My boyfriend turns and smiles, reaching into his pants pocket to pull out a square box. Time stops. Motion around us blurs as he drops to his knee. I've been silent this whole time, walking from the auditorium, to the tree, waiting for this moment. My friends told me they thought he would. We've discussed it. I told him my thoughts on getting married so young, that we weren't ready for this—not at all.

Because in our families, what's expected after marriage? Babies. Lots of them. He's the third out of ten and I'm the oldest out of eight. And I sure as hell don't want that life for myself. I want freedom. I didn't tell anyone that I applied for a job on the east coast to get away from this mid-west hell-scape.

I love Sam. I do. His sweet face, his inability to grow a beard, and his use of the word "freaking" in place of the curse words other people use. The words I write in my journals that he'll never see because I burn them after filling the pages with all of my secret desires. Desires for which I'd surely be punished if my parents ever found them.

"Grace Wright, these last two years have been absolutely amazing. I thank God for bringing us together…" He reaches for my hand, but I'm frozen in whatever state of shock this is.

"Sweetie…" Opening the box, he shows it to me, as if that will change my mind about what is happening.

It's clearly written on my face—I know it is. The confusion. The fear. Two sobs sound from behind me, and I tear my attention away to see our mothers crying into each others' shoulders. After what I'm about to do, they'll need to console each other. Because I can't marry Samson Barnes. Not now. *Not ever*. Not if he wants me to be his perfect evangelical wife. That's not who I am. I don't fit the mold.

And while I know who I'm not. The question remains...who am I? Heck if I know. All I know is that I'm not wifey material.

"I—" I start, backing away. It's then he realizes what I'm doing. "I can't—" I turn and run towards the auditorium.

In seconds, he's on my heels, following me inside the mostly empty building. When he grabs hold of my shoulder and turns me to face him, I'm crying, and he's confused. At least *he's* not shedding tears. I couldn't handle it if he cried. I've seen it once when his childhood cat passed right before midterms last year.

"Grace...I thought we...Was it because I asked in front of everyone? I thought we were on the same page. I thought this was what you wanted. A life with me, here, after graduation. We could finally be together after school."

Together. I laugh at the word. Everyone here knows exactly what that means.

I'm shaking my head at his words, listening to him talk. It's too much. Does he hear himself? By together, he means together, together. As in the pinnacle of man and wife. As in, *we're saving ourselves for marriage*. Beyond holding hands and light kisses, we've not broken those promises we made to ourselves at Bible camps in middle school. But the same hands I've been holding over the last twenty-four months don't hold the same appeal now that they hold a shackle disguised as a gift, no matter how beautiful and sparkling it may be.

"Maybe? Maybe we did. But I can't." I hold firm. *I'm my own person*, I tell myself over and over in my head, knowing that if I falter, I could break my own values and walk out of here the future Mrs. Samson Barnes, for better or worse. And it'd be a fast wedding too—by the end of the summer, I'm sure. On his dad's farm in Oklahoma. Or at my dad's church in Arkansas. They'd marry us quickly and send us to the Hot Springs on our honeymoon for a few days, knowing exactly what we'd be up to. And I won't... I can't. I can't do it.

I won't subject myself to that life. I've watched friends do this to themselves, and watched the light leave their eyes. I've watched friends submit themselves to men and be completely happy with that. But I know myself. I know that's not me. And I won't do this to only ruin his life later.

"Grace... please, sweetie." He's begging now, sinking to the floor on his knees in the empty auditorium. Few lights remain on in the large space, adding more drama to this scene than it needs. Shadows cast over his face exaggerate his frown.

He hasn't reached for my hand again, though. Probably because I've got them held against my chest, clutched tightly in fists, shaking, against my heart that's about to leap out of my freaking chest. Because I'm about to break up with the world's sweetest man who hasn't done a single thing wrong except think that I want to be tied down by marriage.

"Sam, I can't," I repeat the words harder, this time, unrelenting. "You can't change my mind." The only problem is—he can. He could. If I stay here long enough. If I let my family talk me down. If I look into his eyes long enough, those deep pools of blue that I fell in love with might wear me down.

"Then what have the last two years been?" He takes a step toward me, but I stand strong.

I have no reason to believe he'll hurt me. Except that he's angry now, and I've never seen him truly angry...Your college girlfriend breaking up with you on graduation day might warrant a breakdown. "Is that all I get? An 'I can't'? Seriously? I'm supposed to go out there and tell my parents and our families that you just..." He pockets the ring, and then runs his hand down his face, tilting his head back and groaning. "Freaking hell..."

Well, that's a new one—the *hell*. I'll contain that comment, though. Now's not the time. What I can do is tell him the truth, my true feelings.

"I've never led you on, Sam. But marriage? I never thought you'd propose so soon! I thought I'd go off to work, and we'd do long distance, and maybe it'd work out. Maybe it wouldn't. But not this… this makes me feel…caged," I say simply.

"You want a wife—someone like your mom or sisters have been. And I'm not ready for that. I'm not sure I'll ever be like that. There are expectations of us in our families. If you marry me, if I say yes, I think you'll resent me for being different than what you want when I don't automatically conform to your standards, Samson." I don't need to run through the scenarios in my head. I've laid awake late at night, imagining what life would be like with him. And the outcome is always the same. *I'm not enough. I'm too much. My desires will tear us apart.* I step closer and place a hesitant hand on his shoulder. He flinches away slowly with a sigh and takes his own step back, away from me.

Good. Run.

He should. I'm messed up. If he knew what was in my head, he'd know I'm a sinner—that even God wouldn't want him to marry me. He says God led us together. Yet, I know the truth. God led *him* to me to show me the light. Because Samson is pure sunshine. Beautiful. Love. He's everything good in a mid-western Christian boy. And I'm Delilah, there to tempt him into a life of sin. I'm no good for him, and I never will be. So I do the best thing I can, the thing that will keep him on his trajectory to those pearly white gates in heaven.

I turn and leave without a glance back.

Acknowledgements

To everyone who's been here along the way of my writing journey. Whether you've cheered me on, told me I couldn't do it, shouldn't do it, or have just seen the journey. You've been part of this. And without you, this wouldn't have happened. There's so many of you to mention. Here's just a few, in no particular order:

Olivia: Lucille, you, and I haven't always gotten along, but thank you for being the best sister a girl could ask for. Thank you for supporting my writing dreams and reading unhinged smut with me and always trying to be honest even if it pisses me off.

Elizabeth: I don't know if you'll ever read this book. It's not your style. But you've been my writing/book BFF since high school and I wouldn't want to be on this crazy journey with anyone else. Thank you for all of your support and unconditional love.

Sam: Thank you for always listening/reading my unhinged thoughts. You're the Thing 1 to my Thing 2 and I wouldn't have it any other way. You often keep me grounded when I try to fly away.

Nicole, Amanda, Jess (BETA TEAM): I'd be lost without you. Whether it's book recs or early morning/late night international video calls, I've grown to trust all of you with my whole being. Thank you ladies for jumping on board with this project. I owe you the world. But for now, I'll keep singing your praises and leave you this note.

Emily: There aren't enough words to say to thank you for your time and encouragement. Thanks for lighting a fire under my ass and being the gem of a human that you are. The world needs more people like you.

Ambar: Thanks for being a sounding board these last few months. It has been amazing watching you grow as an author. And I can't wait to follow in your footsteps. <3 Keep up the hard work.

Kelly: The moment I met you, I knew you were one of a kind. And the longer I get to know you? It just solidifies that you're an amazing person with so much to offer. AND, you write some amazing spicy content. Thank you for your constant support and advice in this chaotic world!

Alex: I guess I'm buying the steak this time, eh? The day we met, we never looked back, did we? Yeah I was a little scared of you at first. But moving past that, I'm happy to have discovered a friendship for the ages. I wouldn't want to fold the cheese with anyone else. *Hugs and Kisses, GF*

Writer's Block/Editions: Y'all are my people. Laura, Becki, Hannah, Jenn U., Jordon, Marcia, Dax, Avery, Jen G.P.... the full list is extensive and would require multiple pages of thank yous to you all. But you've each come into my life and made it better. I don't know where I'd be on my writing journey without you. I didn't realize that upon stumbling into a local coffee shop and bookstore that I'd make friends for life. And to the people at **Editions**: I wrote most of this book with the help of coffee and bagels and countless hours at the "big table" discussing life. Dawn, thanks for the space to just be me and letting me annoy you and your staff.

Dorcas: Track 3, my Hopeway peeps, I wrote this shortly after meeting all of you. So that says something, right? You gave me the confidence to be myself and come out of my shell some more.

Sidney: You're my lil boo thang. I love you even when we have to use our safe word. Thanks for all of the crazy times and never letting me give up on my dream. It's not easy, but someone's gotta be my friend. I'm glad the universe sent me you. Keep writing and creating.

Elle: My lil baby boo thang. Thank you for working out that scene/diagram with me in the coffee shop. Yes, he can reach her throat.

Cait: Thanks for continuing to teach me the ways of this indie pub world.

About the author

RM Bellamy, AKA Rachel, lives outside of Charlotte, NC with their two daughters. When they aren't napping, reading, or writing their next book, they can be found searching for the next greatest cup of coffee.

Want to connect with R.M.?

- INSTAGRAM: @rmbellamyauthor

- FACEBOOK: @rm.bellamy.2024

- TIKTOK: @rmbellamyauthor